# Friends, Snowmen, Countrymen, Be of Good Cheer

### A Tale of Christmas Time

## RICHARD K. MORRIS

*To Sarah, with love and appreciation.*

Copyright 2019

All rights reserved. No part of this publication may be reproduced, distributed or transmitted in any form or by any means without the prior written permission of the publisher, except in the case of brief quotations embodied in critical reviews. For permission requests, contact the publisher at the following address: rick@listenviewreview.com

*Cover art and inside illustrations by Anne Zimanski*

*www.annezimanski.com*

# CHAPTER ONE

## *Phil starts a Snowman*

For those of you familiar with the colder climates, who have a few frigid, snowy winters under your belts, the process of building a snowman is probably old hat. Who indeed, of those who have spent any time at all in a place where hats, mittens and boots are needed to stave off frostbite, has not tried to make the short, dark days of winter seem brighter by engaging in a little snowman building? Who can resist the friendly face, the plump, round body, and the steadfast ability of the snowman to endure any cold without complaint?

Phil Wellbright could not resist, and so, he resolved to build a snowman. But where you or I would put on the appropriate warm coat and gloves, don our hat and boots and head for the outdoors well prepared, Phil merely went outside clad in cotton shirt and pants, a light jacket, and shoes, and a pair of unlined gloves.

Phil you see could hardly have known what to expect. He did not have a few winters under his belt to guide him; he had not even one. This was Phil's first winter in the north. It was even his first full day in the north; and although he looked forward to spending Christmas in this unfamiliar mid-western town, with all of it's snow, he was as unprepared for the tidings it would bring as he was to build the snowman he had now undertaken to compose.

For this was no shy, first snow, the kind that covers the ground with an inch or two here and there, then melts away after a few hours of sunlight. This was a real, honest to goodness, knee-deep winter wonderland kind of snow. On top of that, it was on Christmas Eve that Phil got his first real experience of it, to really get in there, off the sidewalks and right into the deep.

It was the packing kind of snow, the kind that was heavy and hard to walk in, the kind that soaked through your clothes and gloves. It was the perfect kind of snow for making snowballs, snow forts, and snowmen.

So, Phil Wellbright, in the quiet side yard of a cozy -looking home in a quiet street in a quiet town, leaned forward and huffed and puffed and pushed on a roll of snow of that had grown to more than two feet high. Another man came around from the front of the house.

He paused and watched Phil for a moment. "What are you making?"

"Oh, hi Frankie. It's a snowman."

"*That's* a snowman?"

"Sure, at least that's what it's going to be. Why? What's wrong with it?"

"What's wrong with it? To build a snowman, you've got to start with a great big ball. Balls are round, Curly," Addressing Phil by his own personal nickname for him, Frankie made a circling motion with his finger, "round, get it? That thing looks like you're rolling up a very long rug."

"What am I supposed to do?"

"You gotta start pushing it the other way, from the side, that will round it out."

"From the side? It's hard enough to keep going in the same direction. This stuff is heavy, you know."

"I know. I'll give you a hand. The base is always the hardest part, other than sometimes lifting the head. The two of us should have no trouble rolling that thing till it's nice and big" Frankie took a step off the sidewalk, "If had known you called me over to build a snowman, I would've worn some boots."

"Sorry Frankie. Anyway, that's not why I called you over. The snowman was an idea I had all of a sudden."

"All of a sudden huh? You just couldn't wait to get out and play in the snow your first day, without even getting some winter clothes first?"

"I'm not playing Frankie. I'm not building this snowman for myself. It's for a girl."

"A girl! Already? Don't tell me it's for that honey you were talking to at The Glass Slipper last night."

"No, not a *girl* girl. This is for a kid, a little girl in that house right next door."

"You just moved in yesterday and you're already building snowmen for the neighbors kids? How did you get to be on such close terms so fast?"

"I didn't. I'm not on any terms, I haven't even – hey, what's that about the girl I was talking with last night? What's wrong her?

"Did I say anything was wrong with her?"

No, but I didn't like the way you said it."

"She's all right, I suppose, if you like that type."

"That type? What type are you talking about? You didn't even get a look at her. I just met the girl and we talked for a few minutes and that was all, and you already have her down as a type.  What gives?"

"Nothing gives Curly, it just so happens that as I was walking by where you two were seated, minding my own business, and trying not to listen, I distinctly heard her invite you over to her place to look at her sketches."

"Oh, just minding your own business?"

"That's right."

"Trying *not* to listen?"

"Yeah."

"But somehow over the music and the noise,  standing ten feet or more behind her, you just happened to distinctly hear her--"

"Invite you over to her place to look at her sketches."

"So, what's wrong with that?"

"Do I have to draw you a diagram?  That is one of the oldest lines in the book.  Except usually it is the male of the species who tries it on the female, and it's usually done with etchings instead of sketches, but the principle is the same."

"I know all about that line.  What do you think, that I was born under a rock?  Listen Frankie, you've got it all wrong;  that girl wasn't handing me a line, it was legit.  She is studying art here at the college--"

"So when she found out you were Phillip Wellbright, the famous artist, she naturally saw a good thing and-"

"Nothing like it Frankie.  I didn't tell her my full name, just that I had an interest in painting. The "place" you heard her invite me to was the exhibition hall where a whole bunch of the students' works are on display."

"Oh, well, that's different."

"You bet it's different."

"I'm sorry Curly."

"You ought to be."

"I feel like a heel."

"That's right."

"A blighter."

"A what?"

" A gumboil, a pestilence, a pustule upon the unashamedly uncovered backside of a degenerate, decrepit, despotic, demagogue ."

"Frankie, Frankie, get out of the crosswords would you? This is Phil you're talking to. Phil with the paint brushes and the anything- but- encyclopedic vocabulary. Would you bring it down to my level?"

"I feel ashamed of myself."

"Thank you. I'll say you should feel ashamed. Thinking that nice young woman was out for a quick pick up. I could tell in just the short time we spoke together that she is both intelligent and creative. "

"Yeah, and she's not bad to look at either."

"Yeah and she's not bad to-- would you cut that out? To hear you talk you'd think every man was a wolf and every woman a - a she- wolf."

"I got news for you Curly, if you don't think that way, you're in the minority."

"Says you. You know what I've just realized about you Frankie? You've become cynical."

"Just because I've got eyes does that make me a cynic? I saw the way you were looking at her"

"All right, so I was looking at her. She's a very attractive young woman.

"I suppose you'll say it was from a purely professional stand-point, as an artist. Or were you thinking of asking her to pose for you?"

"Nothing like that Frankie. I wasn't thinking of asking her to pose, and it wasn't from a purely professional standpoint as an artist that I was admiring her, although I could probably just as easily claim that I was. But because you are my friend, my clos-est friend, I freely admit to you that I was admiring her features for a few moments just for my own personal pleasure. Is that so hard to believe? That's all there is to it. After that, I found her to be very enjoyable company, but I had nothing more in mind."

"Nothing more, with a dish like that? Curly you must be slip-ping."

"Listen Frankie, I don't know if I'm slipping or not. I'm just tell-ing you there was nothing else going on in my mind other than enjoying a few minutes company with an attractive, intelligent and charming young woman. Now will you leave it? There just wasn't any spark, that's all."

"No spark? That's what matches are for Curly."

"I'm not using any matches to start any kind of flame unless I'm willing to curl up in front of the fire and stay there. Don't you get it that I don't want to spend a lot of time and energy chasing and making time with a girl if it isn't for real. I've got to feel something, to feel the spark."

"You'll miss out on a lot of fun that way Curly. "

"No Frankie, I won't miss out. I'll make out, because instead of taking a girl out a few times, sure, maybe having some laughs and enjoying ourselves before we both move on to someone else, I gain a friend, maybe a friend for life. That isn't missing out. If I don't feel the spark with a girl, it doesn't matter how good she looks or what kind of a *dish* she is, I'm not going to go chasing after her. It just isn't important anymore Frankie."

# CHAPTER TWO

## *Realizations and Changes*

"Did you undergo some sudden change or life altering experience since the last time I saw you Curly?"

"No, nothing sudden Frankie. This has been coming on for a while.

" 'Coming on'? You make it sound like you're sick or something."

"Maybe there is something wrong with me, I don't know. I just, well, I've never tried to put it into words. Let me see if I can explain." Phil took a deep breath. "When I was a kid growing up in Arizona, all I wanted to do was paint. So I painted, and pretty soon I got a job so I could afford to keep on painting, and people told me they liked the way I painted and I should keep doing it, so I kept painting and I went to school, and even though I wasn't very bright at other subjects, I continued to learn everything I could about painting, and I kept on painting and after I had a degree more people started to like my painting, and then people started to buy my works, and I started to get commissions to do big projects, and before I knew it I was a renowned painter and making big bucks, and more people wanted to commission me to do more and bigger and better paying projects."

"Sounds pretty good, the dream life, Curly. But that's nothing new, I already know all that stuff."

"Well here's something you don't know. This is where I began to realize there was something wrong in the dream I was living. One day I went to check out the location of a project I had a commission on, like I usually do. This job was for was a big mural inside one of those corporate buildings. I'd never met the boss before, and I think he really didn't know much about me either. Anyway, I just showed up one day to study the site, check out the natural lighting, and to see how people interacted with their surroundings when they were actually in the space, stuff like that, so naturally I'm just sort of poking around and watching everything and everybody, and sometimes just sitting there, getting a feel for the space, and that's when I saw the way the boss treated the so-called *little people*. There I was, dressed kind of sloppy like I do when I'm working, perched up on this ladder, taking it all in, when in walks the big man himself surrounded by a whole entourage of people. I guess he must have thought I was a slacker or just some incompetent daydreamer sitting up on that ladder and staring at the walls. I can't really blame him, since he didn't know who I was or why I was there. Come to think of it, it really was a comical situation. But then, instead of giving me a chance to explain, or just quietly moving on and letting one of his supervisors handle it, he bawled me out good in front of a whole group of people; told me to get down off that ladder, get out of there, and stop wasting his money. Then one of his employees recognized me. As soon as the boss realized his mistake he apologized, and after that was the model of a gracious patron of the arts and a successful businessman, but I'll never forget the way he treated me when he thought I was a *nobody*."

"You mean this whole thing is because a guy humiliated you? I thought you were tougher than that, Curly. That sort of thing happens to me all the time."

Frankie gave a shiver and turned up his collar. "Listen, before we go any further, we gotta get you into some winter clothes, and I need to go home and change if we're going to get anything done in this deep snow without freezing."

"I haven't got any winter clothes Frankie, I haven't had time to shop for any since I got here."

"Brother, that's fine. We'd better go and buy you some then."

"I don't have time to go shopping. I have to finish this snow-man."

"Curly, I'm telling you, we need to get into some different clothes, and find some boots too. You look like a wet dishrag, and my feet already feel like two blocks of ice. What we need is some kind of skiing or woodsmen clothing."

"Did you say woodsman clothing? "

"Yeah, sure you know, like *Paul Bunyan*?"

"Oh, like *Paul Bunyan*.   What was that cow's name he had as a sidekick?"

"It wasn't a cow, it was an ox, a blue ox, and his name was *Babe*."

"Oh, an ox, not a cow.  My apologies to *Babe*."

"I'm surprised at you Curly, growing up in the West and not knowing the difference between an ox and a cow."

"I said I was sorry, and besides, I never claimed to be a cowboy."

"Okay, skip it, but we better do something quick, you're start-ing to look like *Babe* yourself."

"How's that?"

"You're lips are turning blue. Come on Curly, we've got a couple of nice stores in town, they can fix you up with everything you need, and I can stop by my place and change on the way.  Of course the stores will be crowded with all the Christmas Eve shoppers, but I think we can still get everything you need and be back in about two hours."

"Two hours! Frankie, I haven't got two hours to go shop for clothes. I need to stay right here and finish this snowman."

"What's the big hurry anyway?"

"I can't stop to explain right now. I'll tell you the whole thing, including about this not being about some guy humiliating me, but in the meantime, come back to the house with me, I just had an idea."

"Well okay, anything is better than standing out here in the snow all day, freezing to death."

They turned and trudged through the snow to the sidewalk.

"At least your walkway is clear, who shoveled it for you, Curly?"

"The agent told me he'd been paying a kid in the neighborhood to keep it clear so the house would be ready to show. He left the shovel for me, which was pretty nice, maybe it goes with the house. Anyway, I gave the walk the once over first thing this morning. I left the shovel in that pile of snow by the tree over there. Remind me to pick it up later, in case I forget." Phil opened the front door and held it for his friend. "Come on in. Watch out for those boxes."

Frankie however, did not have an opportunity to watch out for boxes.

What he had was a glimpse of something furry streaking through the air towards him from the floor, as though it were shot from a cannon, traveling at a high rate of speed, with its intended terminus apparently being Frankie's head and upper torso. This object appeared mostly as a blur of white and brown, but as it grew nearer, Frankie was able to discern the pink flicker of an eager tongue, growing larger and larger as the mass hurled closer. Indeed, for one split second before impact, all of Frankie's world seemed to be a giant tongue. Frankie braced himself for impact. "Oof." he said, as this mass crashed into his chest and proceeded to cover his face with licks of welcome. "Hi Petey, good to see you boy. Did you miss me?" Frankie held Petey up with his arms while the dog continued to welcome his old friend, then the two looked into each other eyes. "Yeah, nice boy, Petey." Frankie lowered his arms and the dog jumped gracefully to the floor. Petey trotted to Phil, touched his hand with a soft nose, and sat down, looking up at Phil.

"Yeah, Petey, it's Frankie. You're glad to see him too, aren't you boy?" Phil reached down and patted Petey on top of the head. The dog answered with a soft noise in his throat, then walked over to the rug he had selected as his personal headquarters, circled once, and lay down.

"You know Phil, I think dogs like Petey could cure half the loneliness in the world."

"Loneliness Frankie? What's the matter, are you feeling lonely all of a sudden?"

"What? No, it's just that, well, the way he jumped into my arms made me – that is, wouldn't that make anyone forget their troubles, to have a dog like Petey welcoming them home every time they walked in the door?"

"Petey's all right, that's for sure. That dog just seems to know, and he's always there, always the same, never gets mad at you or lets you down. No matter what else is going on, or how big a mess you've made of your life, a dog loves you just the same."

"I suppose cats are all right too."

"Cats? Sure, they're all right."

"Of course they're different than dogs."

"Of course."

"I mean, they're all right too, but not in the same ways; cats act different than dogs most of the time."

"I suppose they do."

"I mean, imagine if Petey were a cat instead of a dog for instance. A cat wouldn't jump up into my arms and lick my face, no matter how glad he was to see me. A happy cat, would just walk up quietly and rub against my leg."

"And maybe start purring."

"Yeah, and maybe start purring, if it was a really happy cat."

"Let's say it's a really happy cat and starts purring. Then what?"

"Then I would reach down and rub the little guy, or girl, between the ears and say a few friendly words, and then it would find it's favorite spot, just like Petey did, and lay down. Either way, by cat or by dog, it's a nice welcome home."

"You said it brother."

"So what was your idea out there, and," Frankie scanned the living room, "what gives with all these boxes? You weren't kidding when you said to watch out."

"These boxes are the idea. The agent who leased me this house told me the guy who used to live here left them to be donated to the Salvation Army. The agent hasn't had time to pick them up yet, so he told me that if I would drop this stuff off for him, I could keep anything in them I wanted for myself, so I figured now is the time to take a look."

"Wouldn't it have been better to do that before you went outside?"

"I know, I know, but wait till you hear this story, and then you'll understand why I've been in such a hurry."

"Okay Curly let's hear it." Frankie sat down on the floor and pulled the lid off the nearest box.

"All right." Phil held out his two soaked arms and looked along each one, he then looked down at his pants and shivered, "Man, I am pretty wet. I'm going to shed these things and get into a bathrobe or something." Phil stepped to the bedroom, and through the open door, continued his tale, "Here's what happened. Just listen to this and see if it doesn't break your heart. Last night when I was taking Petey out for a walk, I saw a car pull up in front of the house next door, and then I saw a nurse get out of the car with this little girl, and she carried the little girl up to the house. Frankie, I'm telling you, that little girl must be awfully sick or something. I heard her, the nurse that is, talking with the folks who came outside to meet her, I think they must be the girls grandparents, and I heard one of them say the little girl's mom couldn't be there because she was in some kind of cast, not just any cast, like maybe a broken leg or something, but something big. I remember those two words *big* and *cast,*, and it gave me a chill. Oh, it must have been a terrible accident or something." Phil came back to the living room, clad in a pale blue bathrobe, "Do they ever put the whole person in a cast?"

"I think they do, in the worst cases. I remember a movie once where this guy was so bandaged up, all you could see was his eyes. Only come to think of it, he wasn't really hurt bad at all. The ambulance driver and the doctor weren't really an ambulance driver and a doctor, but a couple of mugs who had witnessed a bank robbery, and they were trying to stay hidden from the robbers, who they were afraid was gonna bump them off to keep them from telling their identity to the cops."

"Yeah Frankie, but listen--"

"So they had just ducked into this ambulance bay at the hospital to hide, when the dispatcher yells out to them to jump in the ambulance and hurry up to to such and such an address, 'cause a guy fell off a ladder. So these two guys figure this is just the perfect ticket to lay low for a while, what with the white uniforms and the ambulance for disguise, when in jumps a real intern and says 'Okay, let's go.' So off they go to the address, and what do you think?"

"I think--"

"Yeah, that's just what I thought, but listen to this. Like I said, the guy who fell of the ladder isn't really hurt bad at all, nothing more than a bump on the head and a twisted leg, but it turns out he is someone they know, and he recognizes them and knows they aren't really doctors and he's just about to ask what gives, when up pops one of the robbers, he'd been following them the whole time, you get it? So this robber's thinking maybe they are the guys, or maybe they're not the guys, and he's been trying to figure it out to see if he's gonna bump them off or not, and these two guys see the robber and they know what'll happen to them if their pal says their names, so they bandage him up from head to foot to keep him from shooting the works."

"Frankie--"

"Then a group of kids come walking along, and they're all arguing about which movie was scarier Frankenstein, or Dracula , and this one kid says 'nuts' to Frankenstein and Dracula, the scariest movie is a tie between The Invisible Man and The Mummy and do you know why? 'Cause of the way  the monsters was all wrapped up in bandages, that's why, and  the kid tells how  he's so scared of guys wrapped up in bandages 'cause he heard it from a gypsy fortune-teller at the fair one time that if you see a guy all wrapped up in bandages it's a sure sign that a witch is about to put a curse or a spell or something on you, and the only way to avoid the curse is to run straight home and wash behind your ears and do something nice for your mother, or else, now get this, you get turned into a toad or something, and how, after telling him all this the fortune-teller puts a toad up on the table, points at it and says that's her cousin Basil who wouldn't wash behind his ears, when *bam*, they walk around the corner and see this guy all wrapped up in bandages."

"Hey, I remember that picture. Right after that, the kids all ran away screaming."

"Yeah, that's the one. You saw it too?"

"Sure, and right after the kids ran away, the dance instructor came along."

"The dance instructor? Hey that's right!"

"*Carmen Carumba*!"

"*Carmen Carumba*, The Brazilian Spitfire. Larger than life!"

"The guy had made an appointment to start rumba lessons that day, to please his fiance, who said he was starting to act like a stuffed shirt and that he never tried anything new. So there he was, all wrapped up in bandages, barely able to lift a finger, let alone take rumba lessons, and there was *Carmen Carumba*, in her crazy hat,"

"And her heels,"

"And her baubles and beads."

"*I am here to see Mr. Phipps, to teach to him to r-r-rumba.*"

Both men sighed.

"*Carmen Carumba.*" said Phil dreamily. "The mystery and romance in that glance.."

"Those eyes."

"The smooth, velvety energy of that voice..."

"Those lips,"

"That poise, that timing, that movement,"

"Those moves."

"Gosh."

"Yeah, Curly. Gosh."

"I'd like her to teach me to rumba."

"Yeah, what a Christmas that would be: learning to rumba with *Carmen Carumba*."

"Yeah."

"Who are we kidding? This is probably the last place you'd find a big star like *Carmen Carumba* at Christmas time. If she isn't at some Hollywood party, she's probably home in Brazil, enjoying the tropical breezes and palm trees; dancing with someone like Caesar Romero, while someone like Don Ameche, with just that glint of mischief in his eyes, watches from a ringside table."

"Really, with Caesar Romero and Don Ameche?"

"Well, either them or some other handsome, suave guys who know how to dance those dances they do in Brazil. All the *Carmen Carumba* movies have at least two handsome leading men types. Not only suave and handsome, but mysterious and romantic too, speaking English, but with enough of some foreign tongue thrown in to give it flavor, and all spoken in an exotic accent. Those accents!"

"Gosh, wouldn't it be great if we were a couple of exotic, romantic guys like Don Ameche and Caesar Romero?"

"Wouldn't it? Can you beat the way girls always go for those exotic accents? What have a couple of mid-western mugs like us got to compare with guys like that?"

"That's one mid-western mug and one southwestern mug, my friend. Besides, I just remembered, I speak quite a bit of Spanish. I suppose that makes me sort of a romantic type myself."

"Yeah, but can you do those dances like they do in Brazil? Do your words flow out like some dark, mysterious river slipping past in the silvery moonlight? "

"Well, no."

"When dames look at you do they go weak in the knees, do their hearts start beating faster?"

"Not that I could ever tell."

"When they hear your voice, do they hear the call of the pampas, the thrill of adventure, the allure of romance?"

"No, I'm pretty sure they just hear a mug."

"You see? You're in the mid-west now, brother. Come to think of it, we're only one mug after all. I always have to remind myself that you're something of a celebrity yourself. I can just see you now, swanking it up at one of those Hollywood pool parties."

"Cut it out Frankie. The closest I've ever been to a Hollywood pool was when I took the guided bus tour of the stars homes that time we were in L.A."

"Yeah, but that was a couple of years ago. You admitted yourself just a few minutes ago that you're getting to be a pretty big name. "

"Listen, there's big and then there's Hollywood big. Just take a look at all the magazine covers at the new stands: whose pictures do you see? Hollywood stars; rows and rows of Hollywood stars."

"I suppose you're right. If you painted a great portrait of Alexander Graham Bell with his telephone, I doubt people would start saying 'Answer the Wellbright.' when they heard the phone ringing. Besides, I just remembered, I know somebody else who's been to Hollywood, He's even worked on some pictures."

"Really, in the pictures?"

"Well not as an actor, but as a musician in the band. Sam Rawlings was out there a few years ago. He even made a couple of pictures with Louis Armstrong."

"No kidding, Sam's that good?"

"Yeah, is he ever. I'll bet Sam knows some of those Hollywood stars, although he never talks much about rubbing elbows with famous people."

"Speaking of famous people, how did we ever get talking about Hollywood pictures? "

"You were asking me about the cast they put that girls mother in, and it reminded me of a movie and I said--"

"The cast! The little girl! How could I get distracted so easily? I could kick myself for wasting time like this. I'll never be able to finish that snowman before dark. I hardly know what I'm doing."

"Take it easy, Curly. We've got plenty of time. I won't be dark for a couple of hours at least. Keep looking through those boxes and tell me all about it. What happened next?"

"Well, let's see. I think I heard something about the kid's father, that they don't even know where he is."

"Must be pretty tough on a little girl like that, not knowing where her dad is on Christmas Eve."

"Mom's whole body in a cast."

"Sick with fever and maybe even, maybe..."

"Dying?"

"I was going to say nausea. "

"Oh. That's pretty bad too."

"But Curly, do you really think the little girl might, might actually be that sick, sick enough to- to, you know, what you just said?"

"I don't know Frankie, I don't know. My sister's got a little girl just about that kids age, and it breaks my heart to think of her sick at Christmas time, with her mom in a cast and her dad gone A.W.O.L So I thought, well, I thought that if I could do something to brighten up that poor, sick little child's day, it might just make all the difference in the world."

"You're right Curly. I can just see the glad expression on her face when she props herself up from her sickbed and looks out one of those windows in that house next door-- probably an upstairs window, don't you think?"

"Yeah, upstairs."

"--and looks out of one of those upstairs window and sees a bright, jolly snowman leaning here and looking back at her."

"Leaning? What do you mean leaning? That snowman is going to be standing straight."

"Not that snowman Curly, not the way you had it started. That snowman would end up looking like my Uncle Fred coming home on New Year's Eve. It's a good thing I'm here to help you straighten it out, and would you look at this?"

"What? What?"

Frankie beamed as he held up a red and black plaid woolen shirt. "Woodsman clothes."

# CHAPTER THREE

## *Paul Bunyan and Babe*

"Well what do you know?" Phil marveled, "Woodsman clothes. Are there more?"

"Are there more?" Frankie reached into the box and dug around "Curly, this whole box is stuffed with woodsman clothes. Look at this, shirts, pants, socks, hats, mittens, the whole works. There are even some boots in the bottom here."

"That's great Frankie, now us two *Paul Bunyans* can get dressed and get back outside, pronto."

"Hold on there Curly, there can be only one *Paul Bunyan*, and seeing as I'm the one who discovered the woodsman clothes, I claim that honor for myself. You get to be *Babe*."

"Me? *Babe*?"

"I'm only doing what's fair, Curly. After all, if you had discovered the clothes, I would let you be *Paul Bunyan*, and I would be *Babe*."

"Well, I suppose that makes sense. Wait a minute, I just thought of something. Oxen don't wear clothes. You don't expect me to go back out and finish that snowman in the nude?"

"Of course not Curly, don't be ridiculous. I'm only saying that I get to pretend I'm *Paul Bunyan* and you don't. Now you can play along and be *Babe* if you like, or, if you want to be a spoil-sport you can not be *Babe*. It's purely immaterial to me which you choose. I would just like to point out that I volunteered to help you with this project, and I would consider it the very limit of ingratitude if you denied me this simple, harmless little exercise in make believe while I supervise and assist in building that snowman."

"Well, when you put it like that Frankie, of course I'll be *Babe*. The way you make it sound, a fellow really has no choice. Ingratitude. Hmmph. But I'm not doing it in the nude; I get to wear clothes, just the same as you."

"Of course Curly, of course. We'll both wear clothes. Everything we need is right here in this box. Look, to show you my heart is in the right place, I'll even let you choose first."

"You will? Gosh Frankie, thanks, that's swell of you. Now come on, what are we waiting for?"

While they dressed, Frankie asked, "So what was all that leading to out there, about the angry boss and all that?"

"I'm not sure I can put it into words, even though I've been spent a lot of time thinking about it. What was that you said just before we came in, 'That sort of thing happens all the time.'?"

"Sure."

"Well, I agree with you, it does happen all the time, to a lot of people. But this isn't about you or I or anyone else being able to take it, or having thick skin. This is about something much more. I couldn't help asking myself, which guy was the real one? If he really was kind and considerate like he was at the end, why would he treat anyone like he did to start with? Then it dawned on me, stuff like that doesn't just happen, like lightning. Stuff like that is something people do. Get it? People *do it to each other.* Do you see Frankie? We *do* it to each other. We don't have to do it: if we can do it, we can stop doing it."

"We can?"

"Sure we can. Don't you get it? Whether I'm a renowned artist with a big name, or just a nobody, I'm still the same person. Nobody is really a nobody, Frankie. We're all somebody. We all matter. The guy at that company just happened to be what started me thinking, but it isn't about him, it's about all of us. He helped me to see what we're all doing to each other, and to ourselves. What's bothering me isn't that some guy made a mistake and treated me differently than he would have if he had known who I was, the point is, why would he, or any one of us treat anyone like that in the first place?"

"Maybe he was just having a bad day. Did you ever think about that?"

"Yes, I thought about that. Maybe he was. We all have bad days. We all loose our tempers from time to time, and do something we feel ashamed of later. Still, I think there is more to it than that. I think we let ourselves in for most of our bad days. I think what finally dawned on me is that the reason people are mistreating and hurting each other and sometimes even destroying themselves so often is because they are chasing after things. I don't mean just trying hard to achieve something, I mean pursuing after things with a kind of obsession that's like a madness. For that guy who yelled at me I think it was the money and the power that comes from being the boss that he was chasing. Then I realized I had to stop myself before I became one of those people. You know, I was getting pretty used to the big commissions. A funny thing Frankie, the bigger the commission for a work, the less of that kid from Arizona with the love of painting ended up in the final product. It's not that I held back, but my name, and the fees I commanded started to hem me in; there was an expectation that each work be a *Wellbright*, and if my vision for a particular project wasn't in that vein, well, I began to realize I was viewed as an outside influence to my own work. Sounds screwy, doesn't it? Then of course some of my wealthy patrons had expectations of what they would get for their money..."

"So is that when you decided to drop out of sight?"

"Yeah, just in time too. I don't ever want to treat another human being like they're a nobody. And I have a confession to make to you Frankie: I was getting pretty full of myself. I think I was starting to feel that because of my success as an artist, somehow that made me a better person. There was a guy I met right after I got out of school in Arizona, another artist. He was a great guy, and talented too, his work was as good as mine, if not better. But there was a difference Frankie; unlike what happened to me, one of his works didn't catch the attention of the right people in the critical circles; then of course I was really young, you know, sort of a new discovery for people to claim credit for putting over, whereas this other artist, he was a few years older, in his forties in fact, and had been plugging away at it for years, with hardly anybody noticing him. So I started to feel like I was something pretty hot, especially compared to this other guy. I started to look down on him, started to think of myself as better than him. I don't mean that I ever consciously thought that, or told myself I was better than he was, but it was a feeling of conceit that was growing inside of me. And even though I never actually treated him poorly, I know that with that puffed up pride and false sense of my own importance swelling inside me, it was just a matter of time. I think he could feel it too. When we first became acquainted, before I was "discovered", we used to have great talks together, about painting, about places we had been, things we liked to do, you know, all that. He told me about his wife, how they met and fell in love, and how wonderful she was. Then after I sold a few works and was on my way, I sort of lost patience for hearing what he had to say. After all, what could an old guy like that who had hardly sold anything in twenty plus years of painting have that could interest a young, prominent, proven success like me?  I was headed for it Frankie, just like that guy yelling at me to get down off the ladder.  We both had everything going our way, and all we could do was step on or over someone we viewed as weaker or less important than us."

"I suppose that's why they call it a rat race Curly."

"Yeah Frankie, a rat race.  We're supposed to be the smart ones, the ones that can figure it out.  Look at us.  Look at the world.  We're not so smart.  Anyway, I had to get out and I had to do it quick.  So here I am  and except  for the real estate agent who rented me this house, who is sworn to secrecy,  you're the only one who knows who I am, or where Philip Wellbright has gotten to. You're my best friend, and I am leveling with you about these things. But it's not sudden, it's been stirring inside me for a long time."  Phil finished lacing up his boots.  "Looks like we're all set."

"Yeah,  we found everything we need in there but some heavy coats. Oh, well, these things should keep us warm enough."

"Okay, let's get going."

Frankie stopped suddenly as he neared the front door.  "Curly, that closet."

"What about it?"

"What about it?  What do people usually keep in closets?  Have you looked in there?"

"No, I guess I was too busy."

"Did you even bother to find out where the kitchen is?"

"All right, all right.  I told you I've had a lot on my mind.  Go ahead, take a look."

Frankie pulled the closet door open. "Wow, would you look at this." He reached in and pulled out a garment of an intense, bright orange such as the boys had never seen before.

"Those are some bright coveralls."

"Yeah, I'll say. Hold on there's another pair in there." Frankie handed the first pair to Phil and reached in for the other. "I wonder why these weren't in the box with the other stuff?"

"Maybe the guy thought the Salvation Army wouldn't take them."

"I guess so. What would anybody want with something this bright?"

Phil shrugged, "I don't know. Hunting maybe?"

"All the hunting gear I ever saw was red, like that plaid shirt you've got on. I didn't even know there was a color like this, except maybe in an electric sign."

"Must be something new."

"No, look at these, they look like they've had a lot of wear."

"Maybe experimental then? You know how these companies are always trying out new ideas. Maybe after they tried it they figured this color would flop."

"Yeah, I suppose that must be it. Well, anyway, we've got them, so let's put them on over this other stuff. That ought to keep us good and dry."

"You really think we need to, I mean, for just one snowman?"

"Curly, I've got a surprise for you. We're not going to build just one snowman. We're going to build a whole snow-family: a Mama and a sister and a brother snowman. You and I brother, and we're gonna make this the best snow-family ever, and we're gonna do it for that sick little girl next door."

"Frankie, do you really mean that? A whole snow-family?"

"You bet I mean it Curly. Maybe we can't heal her mother in time for Christmas, and maybe we can't find her old man either, but we can still give that little girl something to smile about, so I say we climb into these high-voltage jump suits and start rolling some snow, all the way up to our eyeballs if we have to."

"That's the spirit Frankie. I'm with you all the way."

# CHAPTER FOUR

## *Who is Mister R.H.?*

Buttoned up in the orange jumpsuits and glowing like a couple of giant popsicles, the boys started around to the side of the house.

"Hey Curly, there's still something I can't figure out. I follow you about the money and the pride and not wanting to treat somebody like a nobody, but I still don't get why you're not interested in that dish you met at The Glass Slipper last night."

"Listen to you, all of sudden so concerned with inventing a love life for me. I saw you back there, pretending like you weren't noticing us."

"It was pretty hard not to notice with a cute number like that."

"I just thought of something. How could you tell she was cute? You only ever saw her from the backside."

"Yeah, but what a --"

"Frankie! Were you about to say what I think you were about to say?"

"I don't know. You tell me what you think I was about to say, and I'll tell you if you're right."

"Aww, skip it."

They reached the base of the snowman. "The first thing is to turn this carpet roll into a ball. Let's start rolling this thing that way." They leaned forward and started to roll the snow, "So how does all this stuff tie together?"

"Are you still talking about the girl at The Glass Slipper?"

"I'm talking about her and all that stuff you've talking about since I got here; about the angry boss, and everybody being somebody, and not treating anybody like a nobody. How does all that tie in with that girl at The Glass Slipper, and how does it all tile in with you being here pretending not to be you? And what are going to do next?"

"I'll save that last question for last, because that's something I haven't figured out yet. But to your first point about how all those things tie together, it's something to do with the way people treat each other when they are chasing things Frankie, that's how. For a lot of people, it's money they're after."

"Money again. I'm beginning to get the idea you think most of the troubles in the world are caused by money."

"No, not by money Frankie. Money is just a thing. Money can't make a decision, it can't be dishonest or greedy or violent. On its own money can't do anything to hurt anybody. But the mad thirst for money, the lusting after money, and then more money, that does cause a lot of the troubles in the world."

"That's some pretty sound wisdom Curly. You oughta write that down."

"I can't take credit for it Frankie, I remember hearing or reading something like it once."

"Still, you get enough good ideas like that all in one place, it might make people stop and think."

"Frankie, I have a feeling that even if all the wisdom of the ages were written down in a book, people wouldn't be willing to listen to it unless something changes their hearts or their minds, or maybe both. I'm just glad something opened my eyes in time, before I became a slave to my own greed and pride."

"That's easy for you to say. You've already made a pile, and besides that you know your stuff is good, and you can sell your works in a snap if you need to, so you can afford to drop out of sight for a while like you're doing, or even chuck the whole thing and paint strictly for the love of it. Most people don't have that luxury."

"I know Frankie. I know most people would give their eye teeth to trade places with me. All I can say is I'm grateful, and I'll try to help anyone else I can get to as good a place as I'm in."

"You don't have to convince me of that. You've always helped everyone Curly, as long as I've known you."

"Thanks Frankie. Now where was I? This is hard enough for me to explain without getting sidetracked. If I were trying to explain this using colors and brush strokes instead of trying to put it into words, I think I would do a much better job. I feel like you could look at what I had painted and understand what I'm trying to say."

"You were telling me how all this ties together with why you are here incognito, and with you not being interested in that girl at The Glass Slipper. When we were out in California, you would've jumped at a chance to spend time with a pretty girl like that, in fact with lots of pretty girls like that. I still don't get it."

"There! You just said it Frankie, that's part of what I'm talking about, 'lots of pretty girls.' You were right; I would have been chasing them too, just a wolf on the prowl. Don't you get it Frankie? Money is just one of the things people chase after, but there are all kinds of other things too: fame, prestige, power, almost anything you can imagine, even romance. But in the long run, all those things don't really matter Frankie. What matters is the way we, each one of us, treat each and every other person we see in our lives every day. Do you realize how many of the wars, how much of the violence, and the crime, how may broken hearts, how much alcoholism, and addiction, how much high blood pressure and how many stomach ulcers in the world are because people allow the things they are chasing to be more important to them than the lives of the people around them? I can't control the world Frankie, but I can make a change in the world starting with me. From now on, when I paint it will be for the love of representing something beautiful, and when I romance a woman, it will be for the love of that woman. That's how it ties into me not chasing after that girl at The Glass Slipper."

"Don't you think maybe you're taking this too seriously? I mean, so a guy and a girl go out and have a few laughs without either one of them feeling that *spark* as you call it. Is that so bad?"

"Maybe not, if both of them are on the same page, and even then I'm not so sure. But what if one of them is taking it seriously while the other one is just out for fun? You remember that guy that was filling in on drums in that outfit you were playing in out in L.A.? Remember that girl he was going around with? It all seemed like fun didn't it, till he left town all of a sudden without telling her where he was going, or even saying goodbye. The only way she found out he had left her was from some of the other guys in the band, remember that? Remember how we had to sit up with her all night because we were afraid to leave her alone? Somebody finally figured out how to get a hold of the girls parents at two in the morning and we sat up with her all night until they got in from Sacramento? Remember that? That was pretty bad, Frankie."

"Yeah, that was pretty bad. But the girl made it all right."

"Sure, to look at her on the outside, you would never know anything had happened. Then there's my friend Bill from back home. You remember him, don't you? He worked at that dude ranch when you were out there. Remember that cute girl from out East who latched on to him? She used to beg him to take her on long horseback rides in the moonlight. Every night for almost two weeks those two would go out riding alone, and every night Bill would come back with stars in his eyes. He was all set to move to New York just to be able to stay near her, a guy that swore he never wanted to set foot east of the Mississippi River! And she let him believe she wanted it that way too. You heard it, didn't you, all the gush coming out of her mouth every day as she led him around that ranch, arm in arm? That all changed the day she left, when her dear cowboy Bill suddenly became William the hired hand again. 'Here William, here's something extra for you for being such a good guide. Treat yourself to a new hat, or a buckle for your belt.' A buckle for your belt! That kid hit the bottle so hard it cost him his job and nearly cost him his life. You weren't there the day he fell off that chestnut mare, why she was so calm they even let the greenhorns ride her, but calm or not, that mare couldn't keep a man as drunk as Bill was in the saddle. He smashed his head on a rock and spent three weeks in the hospital. The ranch finally took him back a few months later, but he won't let a woman get him alone anywhere, on or off a horse."

"I didn't know he got hurt so bad. Is he okay now?"

"Sure, he looks fine, just like the girl that fell for that fill-in drummer looks fine. The thing is, we can't see inside of a person Frankie, to see where the real hurt is."

"Yeah, that is bad. Still, I don't know what you expect to do about it. You know what they say: *All's fair in love and war*."

"That wasn't love, Frankie. Not for the two that did the leaving."

Frankie paused. "I suppose it wasn't. Okay, Curly, I get it."

"So now will you just stop all those questions about the girl at The Glass Slipper last night? We were just talking, that's all."

"Okay, I'll drop it."

"I don't know why you think you know so much about it anyway. You never even got a look at her face. She might even be somebody you know."

"I doubt that Curly. Girls like that never go for me. I think they can tell I'm just a waste of time."

"Wait a minute, slow down. Girls like what never go for you?"

"Girls like you said when you described her. Intelligent, creative, and charming."

"So you do pay attention to something other than the outer crust after all? All this time you've been holding out on me, letting me think you never cared about anything but how a girl looks in a pair of heels."

"It's not that I've been holding out on you Curly, it's just that a guy sort of feels like he needs to, well, he needs to keep some things quiet, even to himself and his best friend, so he doesn't, well, so he doesn't let himself in for a lot of disappointment."

"Well what do you know? I always had a feeling there was more to you than wisecracks, and here you are, plain as day, just a sentimental soft touch."

"I wish you wouldn't rub it in Curly."

"Who's rubbing it in? I'm happy Frankie. I'm happy for you, and for me, and for the next girl you meet who maybe gets to see a nice guy for a change instead of just another wolf on the prowl."

"Oh, well, thanks. But I gotta tell you, I haven't been giving this a lot of thought the way you have. It's just that listening to you today, and everything you been saying about sparks and sitting down in front of the fire to stay and all that, I don't know, I just had a sort of feeling come over me, like I've been wasting a lot of time chasing after fun."

"Don't go too hard on yourself all of a sudden. You're not wasting time when you make that music. Brother you're good. It looks like you're having fun doing it too, and besides, Petey loves when you play!"

"Oh, I'm not talking about the music. That's all right. That is fun, but that's not chasing anything either. You know, I think I finally understand what brought you here like this Curly. It's starting to make a lot of sense."

"I'm glad to hear it Frankie. I think I'll n need all the moral support I can get."

"So what was her name?"

"Who?"

"The girl at The Glass Slipper. What other girl have we been talking about?"

"I'll bet you think I don't remember her name, but I do, because I have an aunt with the same name. It's Olivia."

"Olivia? You have an Aunt Olivia?"

"Yes, and she's a wonderful woman."

"Olivia huh? I went to school with a girl named Olivia, all the way from kindergarten through high school. Nice kid too. I had a crush on her since I was about twelve, but I was too shy to ever say anything. Olivia. I wonder whatever happened to her? She's probably married to some nice, reliable guy by now. Lucky stiff."

"You carrying a torch?"

"Me? No, I just was thinking --you're aunt's name reminded me of her, and I remembered how nice she was and how such a girl like, you know, so nice, and so smart and everything that, some guy would be bound to fall for her right away, and, and, it just reminded me, that's all."

"Hmm. Sounds like the torch to me." They stopped rolling to catch their breath. You think this is big enough?"

"Yeah, this looks fine. You like where he's standing?"

"Let me see, yeah, she ought to be able to see him from any of those upstairs windows."

"Great, then we'll finish him right there. You start on the head, and I'll work on the body."

"So anyway Frankie, all of this has kind of had me wondering, what happened to us? I don't mean just you and I, but everyone: you used to be a shy kid. I used to paint just for the love of it. That guy who bawled me out probably had dreams of building something great, not just for himself, but for other people too, when he was a kid. What happened?"

"We grew up, Curly."

"Sure, we grew up; we outgrew some of our childish ways and learned how to get along in the big world, but something else happened Frankie, something that doesn't have to be a part of growing up, but something people have come to expect and accept just as if it had to be."

"I suppose we all just naturally get jaded."

"Say that again!"

"I suppose we all just naturally get jaded."

"Jaded! That's it. Is that another one you picked up from the crosswords?"

"Yeah, Jaded: a five letter word beginning with the letter *J* for *weary, worldly, cynical.* But what is it?"

"Right there, pal, right in front of me the whole time, in color none the less. Cynical. Jaded. see the connection? It's the color Frankie, the color. Jade is green, and green is a color."

"I guess you've got something there Curly."

"Yeah, and I want to *unget* it."

"Did you say unget *it?*"

"Yeah, as in get *unjaded* and u*ncynica*l. I think I'm finally starting to figure out what all this is leading to; what I need to do. If there were just some way I could tip myself over and pour all the cynicism out of me."

"Sort of like emptying out a hot water bottle."

"I guess so."

"Then where would you be?"

"What do you mean, where would I be?"

"A hot water bottle only does any good when it has hot water in it. Once you pour all the water out, it just lays there flat."

"All right then, I'll get some new water. Some fresh, clean, hot water."

"Where are you going to get that?"

"Well, I'll just – say what are talking about? You've got me going in circles, I'm not a piece of rubber, I'm a human being."

"Don't blame me, you're the one who started going on about tipping yourself over and pouring things out. Would you be happier if I had said a teapot?"

"You're right. I'm sorry. It's just so hard for me to put what I think and feel into words, and I'm so close to having this figured out."

"Why don't you get your brushes and paints?"

"My brushes and paint? How are they supposed to help me figure this out?"

"You just said the connection is the colors with the words, and that you felt like if you painted it, I would understand what you were trying to say."

"I did say just that, didn't I? Yeah, the colors. I can work with the colors."

"So now we just think of other combinations besides jaded and cynical, and then you sort of paint them."

"Okay, well, let's start by sticking with green. What emotions or personality traits are associated with the color green?" What comes to mind Frankie?"

"An emotion associated with the color green?"

"That's right."

"Well, there's *green with envy*."

"Yeah, that's a big one all right."

"And then there's jealousy, the *green-eyed monster.* Of course green also represents growth."

"It does, you're right. And rebirth in the springtime."

"Maybe this isn't going to be so straightforward."

"Maybe not, but I can't stop now. What are some other colors associated with emotions?"

"Red usually goes with anger."

"Good, good. Red, rage, anger."

"Of course red is also the color of love, as in Valentine's hearts and so on."

"So it is. We'll have to careful with red. Here's one: purple is usually associated with pride. That's too bad, I really like purple."

"But there's also *purple mountains majesty.* There's no pride in that, the majesty represents an ideal, something bigger than us."

"Yeah, bigger than us. That's another tricky one, like having to get just the right mix of pigments, or else you mess it all up."

"Any idea what the finished painting is going to look like yet?"

"Not yet, but I think we're on the right track. It's like this Frankie. I want you to help me to think of all the different emotions and personal qualities and such that can control a person's life in terms of the colors associated with them. Then, instead of trying to pour the cynicism out of myself and ending up like an empty hot water bottle, I'll just concentrate on painting my own character with the colors associated with the goods things and washing away any of the colors associated with the bad things."

"So you want to wash away the negative green and purple, and be careful how you use red?"

"Well, that's the general idea. I know it probably sounds silly, but thinking of things in terms of colors just helps me keep hold of what I'm trying to accomplish!"

"So what other colors are you going to replace the old ones with once you wash them out?"

"Boy, you're really cooking now. Well, let's think of some more positive ones besides love. I know, how about *true blue* for honesty and steadfastness?"

"Yeah, but there's also blue as in *feeling the blues.* There's no sense in painting yourself sad, is there?"

"I'll have to figure out just the right shade, I want there to be plenty of blue, a strong, solid, trustworthy blue. Here's another good one, gold as in *heart of gold.*"

"But not as in *all that glitters.*"

"Right again Frankie, I don't want any fools gold. I'm after the genuine thing, the kind of gold that shines like the light of the sun or with some kind of divine beauty that illuminates a person from within. And then, white. White for purity."

"Isn't white just the canvas you leave blank?"

"No Frankie. This isn't something you just leave. This is something you have to do, something deliberate."

"Okay. Now what have you got?"

"What I've got, what you've got, what we've all got if we just take control, is a start, Frankie. A fresh start."

"That sounds pretty good Curly So where are you going to find just the right shades of all those colors, you know, the true blue, and the rebirth green and the genuine gold, and all that?"

"What do you mean where am I going to find them?"

"You can't just walk into an art supply store for those you know."

"Yeah, I get it. I haven't thought about that. Where do I find them?"

"While you think that over, give me a hand with this torso, then we'll lift the head on and Papa's built. I don't suppose you happen to have a carrot on you?"

"No, and I'm fresh out of lumps of coal too, at least until I look in my stocking tomorrow morning."

"Oh well, I guess those details can wait till later. Hey Curly, hold still for a moment."

"What is it Frankie?"

"There's some kind of lettering stenciled on the back of your suit. I just noticed it."

"What does it say?"

"*Property of M-R-R- H.*"

"*Property of M-R-R-H*? Must be an institution or something. Who else would stencil their clothes."

"Beats me. What kind of an institution, Curly?"

"You know, like the athletic sweats at high schools have *'Property of so and so Athletic Department'* stenciled on them."

"Oh, sure, like a school."

"Sure, a school, or a correctional facility."

"You mean a prison?"

"Yeah."

"You mean were out here in broad daylight in the middle of town wearing bright orange convict coveralls?"

"I hope not. Frankie, do you know of any prisons around here?"

"No."

"You're sure?"

"Yeah, I'm sure."

"What a relief. Just imagine what could've happened if someone saw us and they thought that you and I were a couple of escaped convicts."

"Calm down Curly. You think a couple of escaped convicts would take time to build a snowman right out in front of the whole town, let alone while wearing convict overalls? What kind of dopes would stop to do a thing like that?"

"Yeah, you're right. I mean, even we would be smarter than to do something dumb like that after we broke out prison. It must be something else. But what else? Do any of the schools around here have these initials?"

Frankie thought for a moment, "Nope. Anyway, what difference does it make? Let's just drop the whole thing and worry about it later."

"Okay, but I won't feel easy in my mind till we finish this and get out of these things, or till we figure out what *M-R-R-H.* stands for."

"Relax, will you? It's probably just some guys initials."

"Some guys initials? How do you figure that?"

"It's easy, I don't know why I didn't think of it sooner. M-R is for Mister, and R-H are the initials of his name: *Mister R.H.* It's that simple."

"*Mister R.H.?*"

"That's right."

"Yeah. That makes sense, doesn't it? *M-R-R-H* stands for *Mister R.H.* That must be the initials of the guy who lived in the house before me."

"Must be."

"Kind of strange, a person having his clothes stamped like that."

"I don't know, women have their initials on sweaters all the time, and guys do the same thing with theirs on cuff-links and cigarette cases. And don't forget about all the people who have their initials on their luggage. There's nothing strange about that."

"I suppose so, but coveralls? It seems kind of odd. I wonder if the pair you're wearing has it too? Turn around, let's have a look. Yep, there it is all right: *Property of M-R-R-H. Mister R.H.* Seems kind of strange, having your initials stenciled on hunting gear. All those other things you mentioned are personal belongings, and kind of you know, like a luxury or something. There's nothing personal or luxurious about these coveralls. I can't figure it."

"Maybe he just really liked this stuff and didn't want anyone to take it by mistake, or to help identify these things if someone stole them."

"Stole them? What if someone comes along and thinks we stole them? They've got the guys initials right on them."

"Relax Curly, who would steal clothes like this?"

"Yeah, but we're wearing them. How can we prove we didn't steal them? I wish we would have noticed that lettering before we put them on. Do you think anybody has seen us?"

"So what if somebody has? We're not doing anything wrong. We're just building a snow-family. So our coveralls are a little bright, so what? If anyone asks, we just tell them the truth: that we found these coveralls in your closet. Wearing clothes out of your own closet is not stealing. Anyway, I know I don't look like a thief."

"Thanks a lot *Inspector*, what does that make me, the obvious criminal type?"

"You know I'm just fooling with you Curly. You look just as honest as I do."

"Well, that's some comfort, but not much. I wonder what the initials R.H. stand for?"

"Could be anything."

"Like maybe Robert Harrison."

"Or Roger Hornswoggler."

"I say, *Mr. Harrison*, shall we resume?"

"Yes, *Mr. Hornswoggler*. Let's continue with the snow-family."

"I can't handle being called *Hornswoggler*, better stick with *Babe*."

"All right, *Babe*, let's get started on Mama's base."

"Let's have at it, *Mr. Bunyan.*"

"Hey Curly, I hate to show my jaded side so soon already, but take a look at this character crossing the street."

Phil looked up to see a man approaching them.

"Why? What about him?"

"Take a look at that kisser, would you? Did you ever see such a sour puss?"

"Quiet, he'll hear you."

"He isn't close enough yet." Frankie's eyes narrowed as he watched the oncoming stranger. "I know that look. My shop teacher in seventh grade always gave us that look, even when we weren't doing anything wrong. Looks like you were right, Curly. I'll bet he recognizes these jump suits and thinks we stole them."

"All right Frankie. Like you said we haven't done anything wrong. Since I got us into this whole thing, and just to be safe, better let me do the talking until we find out what he wants." Phil stood up from rolling snow and faced the newcomer, "Good afternoon sir, and Merry Christmas."

# CHAPTER FIVE

## *A Yuletide snowball of confusion*

"Good afternoon gentlemen. Merry Christmas to you too." the man replied.

"Nice day, isn't it? All this snow."

"Yes. You seem to be enjoying it. The snow I mean."

"Oh sure, we're building a snowman. Actually a whole snow-family." Phil motioned back to where the completed snowman stood, and indicated Frankie rolling another base.

"Yes, I see. A whole snow-family. Yes. Very nice. Of course if you want to build a snow-family, it certainly helps to have a lot of snow."

"You said it Mister. I don't know how we could build a snowman without snow."

"No, I suppose you would just have to think of something else."

"Something else? Oh no, that would never work. We have to build a snow-family. For the little girl."

"For the little girl?" The man looked around, but there was no little girl as far as his eye could see.

"That's right. For the little girl. She's sick."

"That explains why she isn't out here in the with you, in the snow."

"Yes, it does." Phil answered.

"Where do you suppose she could be?" The man asked.

"Well, I know she's in her own home, but I'm not exactly sure where."

"In her own home? That sounds like an excellent suggestion. Wouldn't you two gentleman

like to be in your own home?"

"Not until we finish what we came here to do. I'm dead set on that. There have been too

many delays already, and I don't want anyone to try and stop me."

"Of course, of course. I wasn't trying to stop you. I hope you understand that."

"Sure, I understand, but I want to make it perfectly clear that I'm not going back to that home

until I finish what I started."

"Until you finish? Yes, I understand. Well, it looks like that snowman is almost complete. All you need is a carrot and some coal, and maybe some twigs for the arms. I think I even know where there's an old hat you could use. Why don't you come with me and help me find it?"

"Thanks a lot Mister, but we're not building just one snowman."

"Not just one?"

"No, we also want a Mama, and a sister, and a brother. A whole snow-family, just like I said. We've been going pretty good now, but we're not even close to being finished, and I'm not budging from this yard until we're done building this snow-family. They have to be finished tonight, it's very important!"

"Yes of course. I didn't mean to excite you. If you'll pardon me saying so, your friend seems to be having trouble rolling that giant snowball."

"Oh, excuse me." Phil turned and called to Frankie, "Hey, *Mr. Bunyan*, you want some help with that?"

"Sure *Babe.* As long as you've got some clothes on now, I could use a hand."

"Excuse me, mister, I need to give him a hand."

"Of course, but first, did you just call him *Mr. Bunyan?*"

"Sure, you know, *Paul Bunyan.*"

"And he called you *Babe*?"

"Yeah, you know the blue ox. Of course *Babe's* not my real name, I just let him call me that, you know, to humor him."

"And what did he mean about you having clothes on?"

"Oh that? Well, you see, I wasn't wearing these clothes earlier, and I thought he wanted me to dress like *Babe*, and you know, oxen don't wear clothes, but we got that straightened out, and so I put these clothes on."

"You were out here, without those clothes on?"

"None of them. Sounds pretty silly, I imagine."

"Weren't you cold?"

"Oh, I hardly noticed at first, then Frankie pointed out that I was starting to turn blue in places."

"I can imagine."

"Come on Curly, this thing's getting heavy!"

"Now he called you *Curly.*"

"Yeah, that's what he usually calls me."

"Are *Moe* and *Larry* around somewhere?"

"*Moe* and *Larry*? Ha ha, that's a good one, mister. Listen, I'd love to stop and chat, but I really want to get this done."

"One more thing, about those coveralls--"

"These coveralls?"

"We didn't steal them, if that's what you're thinking." Frankie asserted.

"No, no. Of course not" The man responded. "I didn't mean to imply that you had. Where exactly, if you don't mind telling me, did you get them?"

Phil sounded like a defendant on the witness stand glad to clear himself by testifying at last "I found them. In my closet." He said with a nod and a smile.

"In your closet?

"Yes. But I didn't steal them. They were just there. I don't know who put them there, but there they were, and we needed them so here we are."

"Yes, as you say, here you are."

"They sure are bright, aren't they? "He held out his arms and rotated on his axis a complete 360 degrees. "You couldn't get lost wearing coveralls like these, I mean people could spot you a mile off, especially in this snow."

"Yes, I have a notion that was the general idea."

"How's that?"

The man cleared his throat, "I meant to say, I get your idea, about them being so bright and easy to spot."

"Yeah, I suppose if it wasn't for that snow-family we've got to build I would feel a little conspicuous wearing these things." Phil chose this moment to limber up by flapping his arms. He looked like a giant, orange penguin. "Well, like I said, excuse me mister, time to get back to work."

"Yes, of course, I hope you don't mind if I watch. I am rather fond of snowmen myself."

"Sure, sure. Feel free. Too bad there isn't another one of these orange suits, then you could bundle up just like us."

"Thank you. That is very kind of you. Perhaps if we all went back to your closet, we could look for another one of these suits?"

Phil had by some means contrived to get snow stuck to his eyebrows and on the tip of his nose. He resembled an inebriate who had taken a tumble into a snowdrift. "There isn't time for that now, but I'll be glad to try and fix you up after we're finished."

"Of course, just as you say. Oh, look, here comes Officer Carson. Perhaps he would like to hear all about your snow-family. Good afternoon Officer Carson."

Topped off with his cap, his heavy blue coat and shining brass buttons, Officer Carson returned the others greeting while keeping his eyes on the two men in the orange coveralls.

"Good afternoon gentlemen.  Mr. Gordon, I have those toys we collected at the station all ready," He motioned with a sideways nod of his head to draw the other aside, "I wonder if you could relay a message to Mrs. Gordon?"

"Certainly, excuse us gentlemen."  The two moved a few paces away from Phil and Frankie. "I don't think they can hear us over here."

"Tell me what you know so far."

"I saw them here in the snow, pretty much as you see them. They seem harmless enough, but they refuse to consider leaving until they finish building their snow-family."

"A snow-family?"

"Yes, that's right. Not just one snowman, but a whole snow-family.  And they insist they have to finish today."

"Hmm.  Sounds like some kind of an obsession.  The doctors probably already have that diagnosed.  Have they shown any signs of violence?"

"None at all.  They have been completely pacific, except whenever I would suggest that we go anywhere else, then the one that did most of the talking would become excited and say they had to finish their snow-family. They seem almost normal, except for the coveralls of course, which are a dead give away."

"Yeah, there's no doubt about that.  You say they got excited when you tried to get them to stop building that snowman and go with you?"

"Yes, and there's something else.  One of them thinks he is *Paul Bunyan*, and the other seems to be uncertain whether he is *Curly*

57

of the Three Stooges, or *Babe* the Blue Ox. And he says he was out here earlier without any clothes on."

"Jeepers, this is serious. An obsession plus delusions, and no clothes. This almost reminds me of Tarzan."

The incident to which Officer Carson referred was still green in Mr. Gordon's memory. He shuddered as though recalling some horrid nightmare. "The memory of that day haunts me still. I think that I shall never be able to forget the sight of--" He shook his head rapidly, as if trying to do just that, "Oh well, the point is, what are we going to do about these two?"

"First thing is, which one thinks he is *Paul Bunyan*?"

"The dark haired one who looks like he doesn't get enough fresh air. Is that important?"

"Well, if that guy thinks he is *Paul Bunyan*, I want to make sure I don't let him get anywhere near an axe. Just think what could happen if he all of a sudden gets it into his nut that I'm a tree."

"Hmm, yes. I see what you mean."

Officer Carson rubbed his chin as he watched Phil and Frankie. Every few seconds one of them would interrupt their building to fling handfuls of snow at the other. "This is a tough spot." He continued to study the others, "Listen, you go back to your house and call Morning Rise, tell them two of their serious cases are missing. I'll stay here and keep an eye on them." Officer Gordon shook his head. "Look at them, poor souls. Building a snow-family, without a care in the world. I kind of envy them in a way. You know, when you've been a cop for a few years, you see some pretty unpleasant things; the things people do, I mean, and some days you wonder if the whole world has become nasty and mean and uncaring. Some days I ask myself where all the innocence has gone." He shook his head again and sighed. " Seeing those two reminds of what it was like to be a kid, and how nice I thought the world would be when all us kids grew up and changed it. Instead it seems the world changed us. Just look at those happy souls, they haven't got a clue. Why, if it weren't for those orange suits, they'd look just like a couple of poor, dumb lugs who never grew up."

"Yes, but they are wearing the suits. You can see the stencils: Property of M.R.R.H; Morning Rise Rest Home. There can be no doubt about that. Remember *Tarzan*."

This time it was Officer Carson's turn to shudder. "Yeah, you're right. Nobody but the serious cases gets issued those orange jumpsuits. I'll stay here and try to humor them, maybe even try to talk them into coming down to the station with me, but I won't push it if they start to get excited, so just keep an eye on us. Try to let me know how soon the wagon will get here."

"Just as you say Officer, and, good luck." Mr. Gordon turned quickly to walk home.

Under his breath Officer Carson urged himself with an uncertain " Okay, here goes..." then called out to Phil and Frankie, "Well, you two sure have been busy. That's a mighty big snowman you've built there. How many more are you going to make?"

Phil looked up. Small icicles had formed on his hair and eyebrows, "A Mama and a sister and a brother."

"Well, that's very nice, a whole family, what do you know? That will sure be something, yessir. Say, it's getting cold out here. Why don't you fellows come with me to the station? We've got homemade Christmas cookies, and plenty hot to drink. That will warm us all up. What do you say?"

Frankie looked up this time. "You go ahead. We've got to finish this snow-family."

"Sure, sure, you've got to finish. That's a swell idea. I like that idea better than going back to that old station anyway. Well, if you can stand the cold, so can I. I'll just stay with you."

Phil rubbed his nose with the back of his mitten and got some snow in his mouth in the process. "Would you like to give us a hand?" The ensuing snort as he choked on the snow sounded like a man making animal sounds.

To Officer Carson it sounded like a man making a sound like an ox, more specifically like a blue ox.

Training and instinct caused him to to reach to the nightstick dangling at his side. "I think I'd better keep both hands free."

"What's that? I didn't hear you."

"I said I'm not free to help. Normally I love to build snowmen, same as you, but, you see, I'm on duty, and well you know, the uniform and all. I wouldn't want to get it all soaked building a snowman."

"Sure, sure. Too bad you don't have a nice pair of coveralls like these to keep you dry."

"Yes, they certainly do look like they keep you dry. I don't think I've ever seen a set of coveralls like that in a store. Do you mind telling me where you got them?"

Frankie was all prepared with the same answer he had given Mr. Gordon. "We didn't steal them, if that's what you're thinking."

"Why no *Paul*, of course not. I wasn't suggesting that you stole them. It's obvious that they belong to you and that you, well, you have every right to be wearing them."

"Excuse me, Officer Carson, did you just call him *Paul*?"

"That's right *Curly*, I did."

"You know my name is Curly, and his name is..?"

"His name is *Paul Bunyan*, that's right *Curly* You know, if you would think it over and come with me, I think we might be able to find *Moe* and *Larry* down at the station having some Christmas cookies."

"Just a moment please, Officer Carson, I have to talk to Frankie, I mean *Paul*. Excuse us." Phil drew Frankie behind the snowman body and motioned him to huddle down. "Frankie, did you hear that?. I think Officer Carson is missing a few brass buttons."

"Yeah, but I couldn't make any sense of it. What's it all about?"

"Don't you see? He thinks you're really *Paul Bunyan*, and that I'm *Curly Howard* and he wants us to help him go find *Moe* and *Larry* from the Three Stooges."

"Gee, this is a tough spot. Do you think he might be dangerous?"

"I don't know. He seems friendly enough. It's hard to tell with these mental cases. I've heard sometimes they snap, just like that." It was impossible to make the gesture effectively while wearing mittens, but Phil held up a hand and went through the motion of snapping his fingers.

"Oh this is awful. He's a pretty big guy too, and besides, he's got that nightstick. Look at the way his fingers are tickling the handle, like it's just a matter of time before something inside him breaks. What do we do if he starts taking whacks at us with that thing?"

"We'll have to try and subdue him somehow, maybe knock him down. The snow is soft, so he won't get hurt. Then, I'll go get help while you sit on his chest."

"Me? Why do I always get stuck with the dirty work?"

"Well, somebody has to do it."

"Yeah, but you're closer to his size than I am. You would make a better weight. Besides, I know my way around this town, and you don't. How would you know where to go get help?"

"All right, all right. Then you go get help and I'll sit on his chest. What do I do if he tries to get away?"

"Try feeding him some snowball sandwiches. That ought to keep him busy."

"Snowball sandwiches he says. Why do I have to be the one?"

"We already went through that, it's all settled."

"Okay. Only make it snappy, I don't want to have to sit on that cop shoveling snowballs down his throat all afternoon."

"Make it snappy he says. You weren't worried about making it snappy when I was the guy sitting on the cop."

"No, that's because I know how to get right to something, and I know how you always find a way to get distracted."

"Who gets distracted?"

"You do, brother."

"Me? When did I ever get distracted?"

"How about that time in L.A. when a bunch of us guys were all together and we wanted to send someone out for coffee and sandwiches to the cafe around the corner. You said you would go and be back in no time. No time! Must have been more than an hour later when we finally got tired of waiting, we found you making goo-goo eyes and chatting up that little waitress, sitting at a booth way in the back."

As far as it was possible while kneeling and trying to remain hidden behind a snowman, Frankie straightened "I was doing nothing of the kind. I was acting out of chivalry and the most selfless motives. Her shift had just ended, and she didn't want to wait alone for her ride, so I very courteously offered to wait with her. I was not there to chat her up, and I was definitely not making goo-goo eyes"

"Yeah, well how come you had your arm draped around her shoulder."

"My arm was resting on the back of the booth, and her shoulder was resting against it too. My arm and her shoulder just happened to meet."

"Sure," and this *sure* was not one of those quick *sures* that people use when they agree, it was one of those long *sures*, with that rising inflection at the end that indicates the note of skepticism as to the veracity of the statement upon which the *sure* was intended to comment. It was the kind of *sure* that should only be used among immediate relations or very close friends. Phil could just as easily have said *nuts*. "Your arm and her shoulder just happened to meet, sort of coincidentally."

"That's right, more or less."

"Uh-huh. Where was this ride coming from anyway, *Cucamonga*?"

"Do you think I would leave my pals faint from hunger and panting for thirst just to spend time talking with some waitress in that dumpy little cafe?"

"That cafe around the corner was pretty nice."

"All right, so the cafe was pretty nice. But that waitress was nothing special. I hardly even noticed the way she looked."

"No?"

"No. I tell you I hardly even looked at her face, except of course to be polite, and as far as her figure, well I never even gave it a glance."

"She had a pretty face, and a nice figure too."

"Yeah, didn't she?" Frankie reddened, "Hey, what is this? I'm telling you I was only talking with that waitress to keep her company till her ride came."

"Okay Frankie, Okay. I'll believe you if you can answer me one question, because if there's one thing I know about you pal, it's that you only remember a girls name when the wolf in you isn't prowling. So if you want me to believe you, what was the name of that waitress?"

Frankie sputtered like an outboard motor warming up. "C'mon Phil, you can't expect me to learn everything about a girl in just an hour. I didn't have a chance to ask her name."

"You didn't need to Frankie. Her name was Susie, I saw it on her name tag the moment we walked in." Phil tried to contain his laughter. He sounded like an outboard motor with asthma warming up.

Frankie attempted to maintain a dignified silence, but he could only resist for a few moments before he too was making his own sounds of mirth, which in this instance sounded like an over-wrought mule with the hiccoughs.

What Officer Carson heard sounded like two men, man "A" and man "B" who believe themselves to be: A) a legendary lumber-jack who could out chop any man on earth and B:) a legendary blue ox, companion to A) above, or alternate to a blue ox, B1) a member of a famous comic trio whose trademark was physical comedy with hammers, chisels, pliers, and a dozen other pain inflicting instruments that could be hidden anywhere in the recesses of those jumpsuits, working themselves into a frenzy preparatory to running amok.

His fingers gripped the handle of the nightstick, and he paced in front of the giant snowball, peering to try and get a glimpse of what they were doing on the other side.

The raucous noise finally subsided, and soon Officer Carson could detect no sound coming from behind the snowball. This, he knew, could be the crisis.

Meanwhile, Phil and Frankie took a couple of deep breaths in silence. Phil spoke first, in an even quieter whisper than before.

"I'm sorry buddy." He wiped a tear from his cheek, "Oh, if you could have seen your face."

"That's fine. Now what are we gonna do about *Keystone* Carson over there? I hate to cut into your comedy routine, but we can't keep talking like this, what if he wanders off and hurts someone?"

"Yeah, you're right. What do we do now?"

"We better get back there and humor him. Maybe if we let him think he's taking us to the station, the other policemen can subdue him without anybody getting hurt."

"That's a great idea Frankie. And like you said, with all those other policemen around, they can make sure no one gets hurt. I hate to leave off building this snow-family, but what else can we do? We can't let a policeman wander around in his state of mind. I sure hope they have someplace nice around here to take care of a guy in his condition." Phil peeked around the snowball. "Look at him, poor sap. If it wasn't for the uniform, he'd look just like any other big, dumb cluck. Still, in a way, I envy him Frankie. He's not jaded, not cynical like so many of the rest of us; there he is, just believing in his fantasy world with childish innocence. That's what the world has lost, Frankie; that childish innocence. We've got to fight to regain that, and then hold onto it, so we don't all end up jaded, selfish, destructive, lonely people."

"Yeah, but there's got to be some rational ground between being jaded and selfish and walking around believing in fairy-tale characters. You want to have some innocence, all right, but you can't be foolish and believe everything, otherwise you end up like Officer Carson there."

"I suppose you're right, Frankie. Still, there's got to be a way to believe in truth, and to also retain at least some innocence, without believing in fairy tales. Poor Officer Carson. On Christmas Eve too."

"We'd better let him take us in now, he's starting to look antsy. It's almost like he's expecting the paddy wagon to come and take him away or something."

"Okay, here goes. Oh Officer Carson, *Paul Bunyan* and I have decided we will help you go and look for *Moe* and *Larry* at the station."

"You will?" His fingers relaxed their grip on the nightstick "That's great. Say, you'll love the Christmas cookies too. The sarge's wife has been baking all week, and boy are her cookies delicious."

Unseen by Phil and Frankie and Officer Carson, a young child, a girl of about seven had walked along the sidewalk and now stood behind them.

"Excuse me, Officer Carson."

Officer Carson turned, "Why hello Mary Elizabeth. What a surprise to see you here."

"Thank you Officer Carson. Tomorrow is Christmas."

"Yes, so it is. Merry Christmas, Mary Elizabeth. It's nice to see you, but, should you be here--" He cast a nervous glance at Phil and Frankie "Out in the cold I mean, without your mittens. Does your mother know you're out here?"

"No she isn't here now,  but my grandmother sent me out to invite you and these other two gentlemen in for some  hot cocoa and cookies. She just put a fresh batch in the oven. And see, my mittens are right here in my pocket. Besides, if my fingers get cold, you'll hold my hands to keep them warm, won't you?"

"Well, sure I  will Mary Elizabeth, but  I can't come in with you now. I would love to, only some other time.  I really think you should be running along, back  inside your house.  You see I already told these gentlemen that I would go with them down to the station."

"Please Officer Carson, my grandmother will be so happy. She saw these two nice gentlemen here building the snowman and so she decided to make an extra batch, just for them, and then she saw you too and wanted to make sure you came into the house so she could wish you a Merry Christmas."

"Well,   I wouldn't want to disappoint your grandmother.  I tell you what, how about I walk  back to the house with you and wish your grandmother a Merry Christmas, and grab a few cookies for myself while these other gentlemen wait here?" He turned to Phil and Frankie, "And don't worry, I'll make sure to get some for you guys too. What do you do you say to that, *Paul*, and er, *Curly*?"

Frankie nudged Phil and whispered into his ear. "Did you hear that? We can't leave that poor kid alone with a guy that could snap at any second, just like that. What are we gonna do?"

"We've got to think fast Frankie," Phil whispered back, "Just follow my lead and stick with me." He raised his voice so Officer Gordon and Mary Elizabeth could hear. "We wouldn't dream of leaving you alone, that is, to carry all those cookies alone. You might drop some. Besides, Mary Elizabeth seems to really want us to go with her, and her grandmother put in an extra batch just for us. We would be ungrateful if we didn't go and accept her kindness and wish her a Merry Christmas. Let's all walk together, or better yet, why don't you wait here while we escort Mary Elizabeth back to her grandmother's house. The two of us can carry twice as many cookies. Wouldn't that be nice?"

"N-no. As long as you're going with Mary Elizabeth, I'd better go too."

"Are you sure? You might miss seeing *Moe* and *Larry* if you come with us. We'll look up ahead, and you look all around over there, in case they appear all of a sudden."

"No, no. *Moe* and *Larry* will just have to wait. I want to stay with you two."

Frankie put his mouth to Phil's ear again. "The poor guy really seems to like us. I hope that's a good sign."

"Yeah," Phil whispered back, "It almost breaks my heart. I feel just like I do when I have to trick Petey into going to the vet. Look at those eager, earnest, eyes; like some poor, sweet, trusting animal."

"Pull yourself together. We gotta do this. Think of Mary Elizabeth there. Think of all the other people in this neighborhood."

"You're right Frankie. We have to think of them. No matter how much we have to break that poor guys trust, we have to think of them."

"Of course he may not really like us at all. This could just mean he has us earmarked as his first victims when he starts to run amok."

"I didn't think these mental cases made plans that far in advance."

"Sometimes they do. It's what is known as a fixation."

"A fixation?"

"Yeah, like he has to knock us both cold with that nightstick of his before he can get on with his reign of terror."

Phil gulped.

While this was going on, Officer Carson felt a tug on his coat. "Officer Carson?"

"Yes, Mary Elizabeth?"

"Why do those men keep whispering to each other? Are they telling secrets?"

"Well, no, not exactly, not secrets as is *telling secrets*. They were, -er, it's sort of a game with them, that's it, a game."

"I like games. Can I play too?"

Yes—I mean no—I mean, not right now, not this time, that is. You see, they're right in the middle of this game, and it wouldn't be fair to let anyone else in until this game is over. Then, when they start a new game, you can play too."

"Oh boy. I hope it's a fun game."

"Sure, sure." Officer Carson was straining to try and catch some of Phil and Frankie's hushed words.

"What's it like?"

"Huh, what's what like?"

"The game I get to play. Tell me about the rules."

"The rules? Sure, well you see, it's like this, first one person does, no that's not it. First you pick a spot, like that tree over there, and then everyone has to guess, and then, well, I'll have to try and explain the rules to you later Mary Elizabeth, it looks like they're finished." He gave a friendly smile to Phil and Frankie, "Well what do you say, *Curly,* and *Paul.* Are we all ready?"

"Yes," Phil answered "We want to stay together too. We want to walk with you all the way to Mary Elizabeth's house for some cookies, then we want you to take us to the station for some more cookies."

"You do? That's fine, fine. Well, let's get started."

"All right then, that's settled. You know, we really like walking with you Officer Carson."

"Really? That's awfully nice of you. You know, I really like walking with you too, *Paul,* and *Curly.* I suppose that's really why I didn't want you to leave me standing all alone out here. You understand, don't you?"

"Sure, we understand, don't we, er *Paul?*"

"Yeah, we're just a couple of very understanding fellows. So please remember how nice we've been to you, in case you get any sudden urges."

"Mary Elizabeth," Phil asked, "Which is your grandmother's

house?"

"It's this one right here." It was the house next door to Phil's house.

"This house?'

"Sure. Grandmother's in the kitchen. Stomp the snow off your boots and come on in."

After he had finished stomping, Phil asked, "Do you have a sister, or a girl also cousin staying with your grandmother?"

"I've got  girl cousins, but I'm the only one staying with my grandmother and grandfather right now."

"Then who was that sick little girl I saw being carried into the house by a nurse last night?"

"That was no sick little girl, that was me. I was tired. That's why Miss Postelwaite brought me home. Mommy couldn't do it, so she asked Miss Postelwaite."

"Postelwaite? Postelwaite?" Is that the name of the nurse?"

"No, Miss Postelwaite is the name of the librarian."

"Librarian! Who's talking about a librarian? I was talking about the nurse I saw bringing you home last night."

"That's what I'm trying to tell you. That was Miss Postelwaite, the librarian."

"Then why was she dressed up as a nurse?"

"The nurse is Miss Preen."

"Preen? What Preen? You just told me her name is Postelwaite."

"Sure, Miss Postelwaite is Miss Preen. That's the nurse in the play."

"The play did you say? This is all part of a play, and Miss Postelwaite and Miss Preen are all characters in a play?"

"Miss Preen is a character is the play.  Miss Postelwaite is the librarian."

Phil held out his fingers and counted on them as he spoke, "Now, let me see if I've got this straight. You have a librarian here is town, her name is Postelwaite, correct?" One finger.

"That's right Mister."

"And in the play is a nurse, her name is Preen, correct?" Two.

"Sure, now you're catching on."

"And the nurse in the play, Miss Preen is being played by your librarian Miss Postelwaite, correct?" Three.

"That's right."

"And Miss Postelwaite, the librarian, who was dressed as Miss Preen, the nurse, brought you home last night?" Making four fingers in all.

"Now you understand. I knew you could figure it out if I just gave you enough time."

Phil held out his thumb. "But what about your Mommy. Why are librarians dressed up as nurses bringing you home if your Mommy wasn't in some sort of an accident? I heard that she was in a big cast."

"She's in the cast all right. She's got practically the biggest part in the cast."

"Did you say your Mommy was in *the* cast, not *a* cast?" Phil waggled his thumb frantically.

"Sure, Mommy's cast as Maggie Cutler in *The Man Who Came to Dinner*."

"And she couldn't bring you home last night because...?"

"Her part in the cast was so big, she had to stay with my Aunt Alice and some other people to go over some notes on their parts."

"So this whole thing is a mix-up on my part because of a simple thing like a play?"

"I guess so Mister. The play's the thing all right."

"Did you hear that Frankie? The play's the thing. This little girl isn't sick at all. There is no sick little girl. Her Mommy isn't in a cast and she wasn't in an accident, she's in a play! This is wonderful news. To think of all that fuss I was making over building that snow-family for you Mary Elizabeth, when everything is just fine."

"Did you two gentlemen really build that snowman just for me?"

"Sure, that one that's finished is the Papa, and we had just started on the Mama, and we were going to build a sister and a brother too. Isn't that right, Frankie?"

"That's right, Mary Elizabeth, a whole snow-family, just for you, so you could look out your window and see them before you went to bed on Christmas Eve."

"Gosh, that sure is nice of you. Grandmother said you two looked like nice men, and she can always tell."

"Of course now that I know the truth, I mean, I'm glad you're not really sick, and your Mommy hasn't been in an accident, but, brother, was I ever mistaken! I feel like an idiot."

"That's okay Mister, everybody makes mistakes.  Come on in and have some of Grandma's Christmas cookies, that will make you feel better."

# CHAPTER SIX

## *Cookies in the kitchen*

The unmistakable aroma put out by an oven full of warm cookie sheets containing mounds of dough mixed with spices and morsels of chocolate and other tasty ingredients filled the air as Officer Carson, Phil, and Frankie followed Mary Elizabeth into the house. Each of the three men took a deep breath, and the effect on each was instantaneous. Whatever anxieties had been troubling them outside seemed to melt away, like the final bits of snow from their boots, as they stood breathing in the delicious scents that wafted with soothing softness to their delighted senses.

"The kitchen is right through here." said Mary Elizabeth. Whether they needed to follow Mary Elizabeth or just their noses to find the kitchen is a point that could be mooted, but were Walt Disney to animate the scene, it is likely he would have depicted Phil, Frankie, and Officer Carson with their feet drifting above the floor, eyes all a twinkle, as a visible wisp of scent caressed their nostrils and, with a beckoning, smoke-like finger making the familiar gesture that means *come this way*, guided their floating forms to the font of this fragrant fomentation.

"Grandma, I brought Officer Carson and these other two nice gentlemen for some Christmas cookies, just like you asked me to."

At the sound of Mary Elizabeth's voice, Phil blinked rapidly, like one waking from a dream or reverie.  He was for a moment, uncertain of his surroundings, and for a second or two, all he could see was a blur.  Then the heaven of scent through which he had just been drifting seemed to  take on shape and substance, and the figure of a handsome woman draped in an apron, and holding an oven mitt, came into focus before his eyes.

The voice of this woman was soft and cheery, and also clear and quietly confident as he heard it for the first time. "Welcome gentlemen. Merry Christmas to you all. Please come in.  Officer Carson, it's so nice to see you again.  I hope everything is well with you."

Phil could see Mrs. Springyton clearly by now.  Her appearance matched the quality of her voice.  If asked her age, Phil could not have guessed.  His only clue was that she was old enough to have Mary Elizabeth as a granddaughter. Her stature was about five foot four, not an imposing figure by any means, but her bearing was upright, and her body seemed animated with strength and energy and purpose, tempered with a dignified calm that made even the direct gaze of her clear  blue eyes seem above anything else friendly and reassuring.  Her kitchen adorned Mrs. Springyton the way a flowing gown of finest cloth adorned  the radiant figure of a bejeweled and sceptred queen or empress of the Old World, such as Phil had seen in portraits framed in costly gilt wood and hung in galleries.  He had no time to verbalize these impressions in his mind. He merely began a mental sketch and felt a yearning for his paints and brushes and a canvas.  As she had first seemed to him through the mist,  she was indeed a handsome woman.

 Officer Carson stood rubbing his chin.  He was trying to reconcile the conversation he had just heard on the porch with the impression he had of the two men out by the snowman. "Thank you, Mrs. Springyton, I'm fine.  Allow me to introduce my – er friends here, this is *Paul Bunyan*, and this is *Curly*.  Guys, this is

Mrs. Springyton."

Phil and Frankie replied, "Very nice to meet you, Mrs. Springyton."

"Nice to meet you, gentlemen. *Paul Bunyan* and *Curly,* my what unusual names you have. Are you by any chance familiar with the legend of Paul Bunyan, the lumberjack, and his blue ox Babe?"

Officer Carson interceded before Phil or Frankie could answer, "Yes Mrs. Springyton, of course they are familiar with that, but the fact is, we can't stay long, I only, that is we only wanted to see that Mary Elizabeth made it home all right."

"Made it home all right? Why, whatever could you mean by that? I could see all of you the whole time right out the kitchen window."

"You could?" Officer Carson looked out of the kitchen window, and could see the snowman and the yard where he and Phil and Frankie had been, "So you could. Well, that's fine. The whole time we were out there, you could keep an eye on Mary Elizabeth and er, and all of us. Yes, that's, that's fine. Makes me feel a lot better."

"Weren't you feeling well. I thought you said everything was fine?"

"Yes, that's right, but er, when I said everything was fine, I did mean that I felt fine, but that they, that is that--"Here Officer Carson swallowed and paused for breath, "Everything else wasn't going so well, and I was worried, but what you just told me helps me feel a lot better to know that is, that someone like you was keeping an eye out, you see? Keeping an eye out."

"I'm sorry Officer Carson. I don't seem to understand you at all."

"Well, I'll tell you all about it later Mrs. Springyton. Right now, I have to go, because I promised *Paul Bunyan* and *Curly* here that I would help them go look for *Moe* and *Larry*."

"Oh, I get it, it's a game. You wanted me to keep an eye out for *Moe* and *Larry*. I have time for just one round. Do you mind if I make this one up for here in the house?"

"Well you see Mrs. Springyton, we don't really have time--"

"Don't worry Officer Carson, I won't keep you long. I still have all this baking to do. As soon as we've finished, you boys can go and look for *Moe* and *Larry*. Let me see. I have it, oh this is wonderful, I'll pretend to be *Alice Faye*, and you can help me go find *Tyrone Power* and *Don Ameche*, then, after we find them, we'll all gather by the piano and sing *Alexander's Ragtime Band.* I hope one of you gentlemen can play the piano, because I don't know *Alexander's Ragtime Band.*"

Aside to Phil, Frankie said, "You hear that? *Don Ameche's* in again."

"Yeah, I know," Phil whispered back, "Seems like our Christmas Eve is being visited by the spirit of *Hedda Hopper* present."

"Mrs. Springyton, don't you understand?" Officer Carson pleaded, "This isn't a game, I have to, that is we have to --."

"Officer Carson is right Mrs. Springyton," Phil chimed in "We don't have time to help you look for *Tyrone Power* and *Don Ameche*. It is very important that we take Officer Carson down to the station to look for *Moe* and *Larry*, isn't that right Officer Carson?"

"Yes-I mean no! It's very important that *I* get *you* down to the station to look for *Moe* and *Larry, Curly.* Or am I talking to *Babe* now?"

"Babe? What Babe?" Phil looked around. "I don't see any Babe."

"Now, now, *Curly* don't get excited. You know *Babe* is never very far from *Paul Bunyan*."

"Oh, that *Babe*. You're right Officer Carson, I mustn't get excited. None of us must get excited. If you want to talk to *Babe*, you go right ahead. *Paul Bunyan* is right here, so *Babe* must be nearby." Phil turned aside to Mrs. Springyton. "It's very important that we don't do or say anything to excite anybody. Mrs. Springyton. Don't you think it would be a good idea to send Mary Elizabeth to her room?"

"Why has she done something wrong?"

"No, it's nothing like that. Mary Elizabeth has been a perfectly charming and brave little girl. I just thought that maybe it might be best that no children were present. just in case."

"Grandmother, do I have to go?" Mary Elizabeth asked.

"No dear, I don't see why you should."

"Mrs. Springyton, I agree with *Paul*." Officer Carson stated, "I think it would be best if you'd take Mary Elizabeth up to her room for a little while, just until I get these two out of here."

"Until who gets who?" Frankie protested. "Curly, would you listen to him?"

"Now, now *Paul*, no need to get excited." Officer Carson tried to sound soothing. "Just a slip of the tongue. What I should have said is 'Until we all leave together.'"

"That's right," Phil said, "Then we can all go together and search for *Babe* and *Moe* and *Larry* at the same time."

"You gentlemen all seem a little confused." Observed Mrs.

Springyton.

"No, Mrs. Springyton," said Officer Carson, "I'm not the one who's confused. If I could only make you understand without exciting anybody--"

"You're not? We're not confused either Mrs. Springyton." Phil said "It's Officer Carson here, I'm sure he's been working very hard lately, and he probably just needs a rest, and we want to make sure, that is we--"

The sound of the telephone ringing interrupted Phil.

"Excuse me gentlemen, while I answer the telephone. See if you can sort this out....Hello... Oh, hello Mr. Gordon... Merry Christmas to you too...Officer Carson? Yes, he's here, just a moment...Officer Carson, Mr. Gordon is on the telephone, he wishes to speak to you."

"Thanks Mrs. Springyton." He gave a look to Phil and Frankie as he took the receiver, "Now we'll see who's confused. Hello, Carson here...Yes, you got a hold of them, all right. What did they say?...Yes, yes, What? No patients from the state hospital? Said they would check that no one was was missing just to make sure... head count...What!...they couldn't find anyone missing?...all accounted for! Ask them to check again...you did?...Still all accounted for? ...All right. Thank you Mr. Gordon..." Officer Carson hung up from the call. He turned to Phil and Frankie. "I'm afraid I owe you two an apology."

"An apology?" Phil asked, "What for?"

"That was Mr. Gordon on the phone, and he just told me that Morning Rise Rest Home is not missing any patients."

"Did you think we stole some of them?" Frankie asked.

"No, nothing like that. You see, *Mr. Bunyan*, I thought that you two were, say, what is your real name anyway?"

"Me? You mean you know I'm not really *Paul Bunyan*?"

"Of course I know that. What do you think I am, a dope?"

"Well, not to put it too bluntly we did think that you thought that we really were *Paul Bunyan* and *Curly Howard*."

"You did? No kidding? That's kind of funny."

"It is?" Phil asked, "Yeah, I suppose when you think about it, it is kind of funny."

"Yeah, well wait to you hear something else and see if you think this is funny, 'cause I thought that you two thought that you really were *Paul Bunyan*, and *Curly Howard*. Except I also thought that you sometimes thought you were *Babe* the blue ox."

"*Curly Howard* and *Babe* the blue ox?"

"Yeah, sort of a split split personality. You've no idea what a relief this is. I kept worrying if I was gonna be able to get you guys to the station without any trouble. I could tell you didn't mean any harm, and I really didn't like the idea of having to konk one of you on the head with this nightstick if you got out of hand."

"That's some relief to me too." Said Frankie, rubbing the back of his head.

"Yeah, same goes for me." said Phil. "We were worried what to do if you snapped all of a sudden just like that and started going after people with that thing."

"Oh no, that would be strictly against regulations."

"Yes, but you have to remember, at the time, we thought you were crazy." Phil replied

"Oh, well that's different."

"Yeah, so we decided we would have to knock you down, and then I was gonna go for help, while Curly here sat on your chest to keep you from getting away." said Frankie.

"No Frankie, I was going to go for help and you were to stay and sit on his chest."

"That's what you said at first, but then I pointed out that you wouldn't know where to run for help, this being your first day in town, and besides you're bigger than I am and would make a better weight, so we agreed I was gonna run for help and you were gonna sit on his chest. Remember?"

"That's right, so we did. Officer Carson, Frankie was going to run for help while I sat on your chest."

"And shoveling snowball sandwiches down your throat if you tried to get away."

"Yes, that too; and shoveling snowball sandwiches down your throat if you tried to get away."

"I'm sure glad you guys didn't try anything like that. Striking an officer and impeding him in the performance of his duty, those are serious matters. You could have gotten into a lot of trouble."

"Really?" Asked Frankie, "About how much trouble?"

"Oh, I don't know, let's see, probably ninety days, maybe six months."

"Don't forget about the snowball sandwiches." Frankie added, like a parent helping a child figure a story problem in math.

"Hmm, yeah, snowball sandwiches. I don't know if there's anything in the penal code about snowball sandwiches. How many sandwiches are we talking about?"

Frankie shrugged. "Depends on how hard you struggled."

"I don't give up easily."

"No? Better make it a dozen."

"A dozen eh? "Officer Carson cleared his throat and thought for a moment, "I'd say to be on the safe side, we'd better make it six months to a year."

"You sure? A dozen is twelve. Twelve months in a year. Doesn't that kind of just go together?"

"You're right. Better make it a solid year, with time off for good behavior."

"You hear that Curly? What a close call you almost had. I sure would have missed you brother."

"Missed me? What are you talking about? You would be right there with me."

Frankie shook his head, "Uh-uh. I only helped knock him down. You were the one who sat on his chest and stuffed him full of snow. They'd probably let me off with about thirty days. What do you say Officer Carson, does thirty days sound about right?"

"Well, let's see, subtract the time for sitting on the chest and the snowball sandwiches, taking into account for a first offense— this is your first offense, isn't it?"

"Officer Carson, do I look like the criminal type to you?"

Officer Carson looked at Frankie, held his breath a moment, and cleared his throat, "We'll just let that pass and say it was your first offense. So, taking everything into consideration, I would say, yes, you are probably pretty close. I think you would get thirty days, and he would get the full twelve months."

"With time off for good behavior. Don't forget that." Frankie patted Phil on the shoulder. "We do want to encourage him to have good behavior."

"As you say, with time off for good behavior."

Frankie turned both hands palms up, "You see Phil, you'd been in there for the full year, while I'd be out in thirty days. It's an open and shut case."

Phil's face had taken on a reddish hue by now, "Wait a minute, wait a minute. You guys are getting carried away, so just slow down a minute or the next thing I know you'll have me doing ten years in Alcatraz. Now Officer Carson, I don't mean to doubt your knowledge of the laws of this state, but I must ask for your attention while I remind you of one simple fact."

"Sure, what's that?"

"We thought you were crazy at the time! Not only crazy, but liable to snap at any moment, just like that, and run amok with that nightstick of yours, taking whacks at people and causing general panic and confusion."

"Oh, yes, well, I suppose if you testify that you thought I was crazy, that would be of material interest to the court. Yes, I suppose that may cause the judge to reduce your sentence."

"Meanwhile, what about you? Would you have anything to say that might be of material interest to the court?"

"Me? Why I could… say, I could tell the judge that the whole thing was just a big mix-up, that you guys didn't mean any harm at all, and that I thought you were just as crazy as you thought I was. Why that should make a big difference, yessiree! In fact, I think you guys might even get off with a stern warning from the bench."

"You hear that Frankie? A stern warning from the bench." Phil crossed his arms in front.

"What's to complain about? We can't beat that."

"We? You were trying to send me up for twelve months, when Officer Carson here, who ought to know, once he considers all the facts, says I should only get a stern warning from the bench."

"I was just trying to show you that crime doesn't pay. You should know better than to sit on a policeman's chest and shove snowball sandwiches down his throat."

Phil's voice was now the loudest his sense of the proprieties would allow him to use as a guest in someone's house, "I do know better than to sit on a policeman's chest and shove snowball sandwiches down his throat. The only reason I was going to sit on his chest in the first place was if he snapped just like that, and to hold him down while you ran to get more policeman. As for shoving snowball sandwiches down his throat, that was your idea. Did you get that Officer Carson? The snowball sandwiches were his idea, not mine. Off all the screwball notions, I would have never dreamed of shoving snowball sandwiches down your throat if my best friend here hadn't put the crazy idea--" Phil broke off. It was as if some sudden, pressing question had just burst into his mind.

Phil resumed in a much more quiet, calm voice. "Officer Carson, what first gave you the idea that Frankie and I were crazy?"

"You mean you don't know?" He asked with raised eyebrows.

Both Phil and Frankie raised their eyebrows too, and shook their heads as well.

Officer Carson looked from one to the other taking in their response. His eyebrows returned to the starting position. "It's the orange coveralls."

"These? I'll admit they do pretty much grab the eyes, but isn't that the point of hunting gear?"

"Those aren't hunting coveralls. Turn around, I'll show you. Here it is, stenciled right across your back: *Property of M-R-R-H.*"

"Sure, we saw that, but we couldn't figure out what it meant, other than some guys initials."

"Some guys initials? What kind of a person would stencil his initials on coveralls like these?"

"Just what I asked him myself, Officer Carson. You remember Frankie? And you started in with all that stuff about ladies sweaters, and cuff links and things."

Frankie took up his defense. "Look, it's simple? M-R-R-H. We figured the M-R was for Mister, and the R-H were his initials. Mr. R.H. Except we don't know anything about him but that."

"Listen you guys, M-R-R-H. is not a person, it's a place: Morning Rise Rest Home, it's just a few miles outside of town."

"A rest home, you mean for people who've had nervous breakdowns and stuff like that?"

"Yeah, mostly stuff like that. But every once and a while they have to take a patient from the State mental hospital."

"The mental hospital? So you thought we were a couple of patients from the State mental hospital?"

"Yeah, the orange coveralls were a dead giveaway. Morning Rise only issues those to the transfers from the State mental hospital."

"That's right," Mrs. Springyton said, "Like that poor gentleman who thought he was Tarzan. You were very brave, Officer Carson. I don't think this town will ever forget what you did that day."

"That's what I'm afraid of."

"Afraid? Of what?"

"That no one will forget. If it's all the same to you, I'd rather everyone just developed amnesia about that whole Tarzan incident."

"You're so modest. Amnesia, that's just what started whole thing too. However, just as you say. But I still say you acted very bravely."

"Yes, well, thank you Mrs. Springyton. Now, where were we?"

"You were just telling Curly and I why you thought we were a couple of nuts."

"Yes, that's right. Like I said, they only issue those orange coveralls to the transfers from the State hospital, so naturally when I saw you two out there in the snow, obsessed with finishing that snow-family, and calling each other names like *Paul Bunyan* and *Curly*, making all kinds of strange noises, and on top of everything else, wearing those coveralls, I just thought you two were --"

"Off our rockers." Frankie finished.

"Yes. Of course, nuts and crazy and off your rockers isn't the correct technical language. In my report I would probably have to use words like obsessive behavior and delusional and a whole bunch of other three dollar words like that. Out here on the beat, just between us regular people, crazy works just as well, and it doesn't take as long."

"Yeah, and it's a lot easier to spell." Frankie added.

"You don't have to remind me of that. You know what I want for Christmas? A Webster's Dictionary, of my very own. We've got one of those five and dime store pocket-sized jobs down at the station that me and the other fellows all share, but I always feel like a dope every time I look something up in front of the other guys. I want one of those big, hard cover Websters, as thick as a triple-decker sandwich, with extra tomato, and I want to learn all the really tough words at home, so that when I fill out my reports at the station, I don't have look the words up in front of the other guys. As long as I can remember them that is."

Frankie's face lit up, "You should do what I do and work the crosswords. That's how I remember how to spell. First I look them up, then I write them down. It's a great system, and working the puzzles keeps it from being a bore."

"The crosswords? Yeah, that's a swell idea. Thanks a lot."

"Don't mention it. Another great thing about doing that is as long as you're looking up the spelling of the words, you might as well learn what they mean. Having a dictionary and working the crosswords has improved my vocabulary extensively."

"Has it really?"

"You bet. And I enjoy that part of it too. You know a lot of people wouldn't think it to look at me, but I'm really quite a philologer."

"Please, not while there are ladies present."

"Oh, that's okay. You see, a philologer is a person who is expert in, or loves the study of words." Frankie turned to Mrs. Springyton "I apologize if you think I was getting out of line."

"That's quite all right. Although I didn't know the meaning of that word until you told us, I was quite certain that a fine young man like yourself wouldn't use any offensive language in front of a young child."

Frankie reddened, "No, of course not." This time he turned to Mary Elizabeth, "Mary Elizabeth, you did hear the meaning of that big word I used didn't you?"

"Sure," the child answered, "A person who is expert in, or loves the study of words."

"That's right. You sure do pay attention."

"Thank you Mister. Mommy told me children should always pay attention to what their elders say, so I make sure to listen very closely whenever grown-ups are speaking."

"That's fine, Mary Elizabeth. I'm sure your mommy will be very pleased with you. Speaking of paying attention, I hope you understand that I was joking a little while ago when I was talking about going to jail."

"Sure, I could tell you were joking. It was really funny, but I didn't laugh because I didn't want to spoil it. I could tell Officer Carson and the other nice gentleman were taking you seriously. You sure tell a funny story."

"Well, thanks for not ruining the gag. I'll remember next time to run my jokes past you first, to see if you think they're funny too."

"Okay Mister, I like jokes, but there is something I wish you would tell me first."

"What's that?"

"What are we supposed to call you?"

"To call us?"

"Yes. If your name isn't really *Paul Bunyan* and  and the other gentleman's name isn't really *Curly Howard*,  what are we supposed to call you?"

"Sure Mary Elizabeth.  My real name is Frankie Elliot, you can call me Frankie, or Mr.  Elliot if you like, and my friend here is Phil...er.." Frankie cast a questioning look at Phil.

"Phil, er, Webster." Phil said.

"I didn't quite catch that, did you say Webster? "asked Officer Carson.

"That's right, Webster. Just like the dictionary."

"Well, what do you know?"

"Yes, quite a coincidence isn't it?"

"Well, it's nice to meet you two. For real this time, I mean."

Mrs. Springyton placed a large tray with an assortment of Christmas cookies on the kitchen table, followed by another tray with four cups of steaming cocoa.

"Well, now, Mr. Elliot, Mr. Webster, and Officer Carson, as soon as you've finished laughing,  perhaps  you would care for some cookies? Be careful, I think the cocoa is still very hot"

Being a small child  has it's advantages, especially when there are trays of cookies set out on tables.  Just inches below her face, the whole array seemed to stretch on for miles before Mary Elizabeth's wide and wondering eyes. Cookies of every imaginable description were stacked high and wide, here a simple drop, there a bar, over there  a star, a tree and  even a tin soldier! Some were plain, some were frosted, others had a powdery coating that looked like snow, and still others glistened with tiny sparkles of green and red and gold. There were the familiar chocolate chip cookies, their sweet and tender shapes bulging with the morsels of chocolate within, and others were not quite so familiar, but seemed part of the vague and fantastic treasures of the few Christmas' stored within Mary Elizabeth's memory: some she had seen perhaps only once before, and a year is such a long time in the life of a child. Among these were one type that caught Mary Elizabeth's attention and held her spellbound; they were formed by some unknown craft of her grandmother into a swirl of chocolaty looking brown and toasty, rich tan. "May I have some too, Grandmother?"

"Yes, dear, but only one cookie, it's getting close to dinner time. Officer Carson, there are some chocolate chip, I believe they are your favorites. I took them out of the oven only a few moments before you gentlemen came in."

"Chocolate chip? Just out of the oven?" Officer Carson took one and held it up, like someone proposing a toast, "Gentleman, I think you'll agree that few things in life are more enjoyable than a chocolate chip cookie that is still warm and gooey from the oven."

"Here here." Agreed Frankie, reaching for one.

Phil pondered aloud, "Well now, they all look so good. This is not going to be an easy choice. Mary Elizabeth, what would you suggest?"

"If I were going to have two, I would start with a chocolate chip, just like everyone else. Like Officer Carson said, there's nothing quite like a chocolate chip cookie still warm and gooey from the over. Better get them while they're warm if you've got the chance."

"Sound advice. What would be your next choice?"

"I would take one of those." Mary Elizabeth indicated the swirl cookies.

"M'yes, those look very good too." Phil stroked his chin as he eyed the cookies, "I guess I'll do as you suggest and start with the chocolate chip. As you say, better get them while they're warm, if you've got the chance."

Officer Carson finished a thoughtful mouthful of cookie, "I'm surprised you two didn't know what people would think when they saw you wearing those orange jumpsuits. Every one in town must know about Morning Rise."

"There's a very simple explanation for that. I just arrived in town yesterday." Phil answered. "I've never been here before."

"What about you, Mr. Elliot, you're from around here aren't you?"

"Yeah, sure. I grew up here, but I've been away for a few years. I guess in the excitement of getting Phil settled in, and wanting to help him build that snow-family, I just forgot."

"Well, no harm done. But seriously, if you didn't get them at Morning Rise, where did you get them?"

"We found them in the closet of the house I'm renting. I'm from Arizona and don't have any winter clothes yet, and Frankie here wasn't dressed for tromping around in the snow. We found a whole box of winter clothes that the previous tenant of the house left to take to the Salvation Army but we found the coveralls in the closet. I guess he knew they would cause a lot of confusion if someone picked them up from the Salvation Army."

"We had a next door neighbor named Bill Travers who worked at Morning Rise." said Mrs. Springyton. "I remember he said they gave him some of the surplus coveralls, because they really are rarely ever needed. I believe he and his brother used to wear them went they went up north. He moved away not long ago. I wonder if he's having a nice Christmas?"

"Then you must have known that Frankie and I weren't really patients from Morning Rise."

"Must I have? Why?"

"Because I just moved into the house next door. Those must have been the coveralls your friend Bill Travers had. He must have left them behind."

"Why of course! Bill Travers must have left them behind, that explains everything. But you say you just moved into the house next door? Good gracious. I must apologize for not getting over with James, that's Mr. Springyton, and giving you a proper welcome. No one should have to feel like a stranger in their own neighborhood. I do hope you'll forgive me, Mr. Webster."

"That's quite all right Mrs. Springyton, there's nothing to forgive. Besides, you probably know how we unmarried men don't mind if we miss out on those kind of niceties. You know, the carefree life and all that."

"Oh yes, I know about all that. That's why you need someone to watch after you."

"Oh I don't know, some of us seem to do all right watching out for ourselves, don't we Frankie?"

"You've got some chocolate on your chin, Curly."

"Oh, thanks." Phil wiped his chin with a napkin, "Anyway, Mrs. Springyton, are you saying that you didn't know that I had moved into the house next door? That just earlier today, dressed as we are, was the first time you have seen me?"

"Yes, that's right."

"And so you thought that Frankie and I were really patients from Morning Rise who had wandered off somehow?"

"Yes. I recognized the coveralls, just like Officer Carson. I hope you'll forgive me for jumping to conclusions."

"That's all right, Mrs. Springyton. But, you thought we were really patients from the rest home, and yet you invited us in to your home, you even started an extra batch of cookies for us, before Officer Carson arrived to make sure it was, well, to make sure we behaved ourselves. Weren't you concerned?"

"Of course I was. That's why I invited you in. I saw you two gentlemen out there in the snow, and I thought, if that was someone in my family, some person I loved, I would want someone to offer them kindness, and a place to come in out of the cold."

Phil couldn't respond right away. He gazed at Mrs. Springyton, then looked at Frankie, who returned his look of wonder.

"You didn't even know us, you even thought we were patients from a mental institution and yet you…? But what about Mary Elizabeth, weren't you concerned for her, or for yourself?"

"Good heavens no. I asked Mary Elizabeth to go out only after I saw that Officer Carson had arrived. I could tell by the actions of all three of you that there was no cause for alarm. I just saw two kind and gentle looking men who appeared to be lost, who needed someone to provide them rest and warmth. I did what I would do for any neighbor."

"Neighbor? But I thought you said you didn't know I had moved into the house next door."

"I didn't mean neighbor as in someone who lives near me. Any person who is affected by my actions is my neighbor."

"That includes a lot of people in some way or another, Mrs. Springyton."

"Yes, I suppose it does."

"Isn't that kind of hard to do, worrying about how to treat so many people?"

"Good gracious no. I never worry about it; I just do the right thing."

# CHAPTER SEVEN

## *A heart of gold*

Officer Carson finished a soothing sip of cocoa and asked. "There is one thing I still don't understand. Why were you two so determined to complete that snow-family of yours today? When I asked you to come to the station with me, you dug in your heels like a couple of mules. What was up with that?"

"Officer Carson, I'm afraid that is a rather long and sad story, long because it takes a while to tell, and sad because you see before you the sad sap who has made a complete fool of himself. It all started last night, while I was out walking my dog Petey. I happened to be on the sidewalk in front of the Springyton's house when I saw a woman dressed as a nurse carrying what I supposed to be a sick little child into the house. Then I heard Mr. and Mrs. Springyton speaking to the *nurse* about a big cast of some kind, and, well I imagined the sick little girl's mother had been in some sort of terrible accident, and was in a big cast. Then I heard someone say they didn't know where Mary Elizabeth's father was, or if he would be home for Christmas. I thought he had skipped out on his own family." He turned to Mrs. Springyton. "I suppose I was wrong about that too?"

"Yes, my son-in-law is in the Navy. We found out only today that he will be coming home to spend Christmas with us."

"Well, I'm glad to hear that. Anyway, so here I was, the night before Christmas Eve, and here was this poor, sick little girl, her mother in a bed of pain after suffering some terrible injuries, and her irresponsible father nowhere to be found. I wanted to do something to cheer the little girl up, to brighten what I thought was going to be a pretty sad Christmas for her, so I decided to build a snowman for her, and that it had to finished before it got dark on Christmas Eve."

"So what made you decide to build more? When I got there, you already had the one snowman built."

"That's because Frankie here decided to help. You see, I've never spent a winter in the north, in fact I've never built a snowman, so when Frankie heard my story about the sick little girl, he offered to help, and even insisted we build a whole snow-family for her sake."

"That is so sweet of you gentlemen. It really shows what kind and generous natures each of you has."

"Thank you Mrs. Springyton. Well, just to conclude the tale of my misadventure," Phil continued, "Mary Elizabeth cleared the whole thing up for me just before we came inside the house. I now know that the lady I saw in the nurses uniform was your librarian dressed as her character in the play you are doing in town, and that you daughter, Mrs, Springyton, is also in the cast of that play, not in a cast as a result of some accident."

"It was an innocent mistake, and you meant well, and besides nobody has suffered any harm. In fact, hasn't this all really worked for our own good, to bring us close together like this, when we might still be practically strangers? I'm glad to have you as a neighbor Mr. Webster. Both of you must feel free to stop in as often as you like."

"Thank you Mrs. Springyton. Curly and I are great pals, so I'm sure I'll be around. These cookies are delicious, do you mind if I have another?"

"Help yourself. Please, everybody, help themselves. Officer Carson, are you leaving so soon?"

"I'd love to stay and visit with you Mrs. Springyton, but everything is all right here and I'm still on duty, so I'd better be going. Thanks for the cookies and cocoa."

"We should be going too, Mrs. Springyton. I want to change out of these coveralls before we create any more confusion. Thank you for your hospitality. You have a lovely grand-daughter."

"Thank you Mr. Webster. It's too bad you didn't get a chance to meet the rest of the family, but my husband is meeting our son-in-law Robert, and a visitor, a Mr. *Li*, at the station, and my daughters are both at the theatre."

"Oh, you have more than one daughter in the play?"

"Yes, my younger daughter Alice is in the show too."

"Well, perhaps we'll get to meet them all soon."

"Mr. *Lee*," Frankie queried, "would that be one of the *Lees* of Virginia?"

"No, as a matter of fact, I believe he is one of the *Lis* of China."

"China?!" All three men chimed together.

"Yes, Robert said he was on some sort of diplomatic mission, and was assigned as the host and liaison for an important visitor from China. That's really all I know about the whole thing, but I do think it sounds rather exciting."

"Yes." Phil agreed. "I suppose that does sound rather exciting, hosting a diplomatic envoy."

"Exciting and mysterious. All the way from China, no less" Frankie added.

"Well, we'll all get to meet this Mister Li tonight. You gentlemen are welcome to call back after you get settled. Same to you Officer, whenever your duty permits."

They all thanked her, everyone said goodbye, and Phil, Frankie, and Officer Carson stepped out into the late afternoon air.

"Officer Carson," Phil said "I gathered from your remarks inside that the story having to do with Tarzan is something you would rather not discuss, but, seeing as we all seem to be connected by circumstances to that fateful event, I would appreciate if you would tell us about it."

"Okay, I guess you guys have a right to know. It's like I told you inside, Morning Rise is really just a home for people who need peace and quiet. They have doctors and a professional staff and all that, but they really aren't set up to deal with serious mental cases. Sometimes though, Morning Rise has to take patients from the State mental hospital, if they are short of beds, or if someone needs to be moved to another location; it's only ever been temporary, two or three days at the most. Some of these cases though can be pretty tough, so the doctors and directors at Morning Rise realized it would be best to issue those orange coveralls, to help everyone keep alert to their whereabouts. One day a fellow was transferred to Morning Rise who was suffering from complete amnesia. Poor guy didn't know where he was from, if he had any family, not even his own name. To make matters worse, he was under the delusion that he was Tarzan of the jungle. His first night he gets out of Morning Rise and ends up right here in the middle of town. So what does he do? Strips down naked to his underwear."

"What a shocking development. Did anyone see him?" Frankie asked.

"Did they? Brother, practically the whole town saw him. This guy was no Johnny Weissmuller either, let me tell you. He was sort of round and tubby, looked more like a potato with arms and legs than a guy who could swing from vine to vine and wrestle crocodiles."

"What happened next?"

"No sooner do a couple of guys see him than he starts pelting them with apples, twigs, rocks, anything he could lay his hands on."

"Pelting them? Why would Tarzan do a thing like that."

"Think. He didn't have a knife, or any kind of a weapon, so he used what he could find. There happen to be a few apple trees in town near the library, so they provided him with most of his ammunition."

"But why? Why pelt the men at all? Didn't Tarzan usually help people?"

"Because he thought they were ivory hunters, come to exploit the graveyard of the elephants. He kept yelling '*Me Tarzan, white hunters go away.*' Tarzan thought all the men who looked like himself where either ivory poachers or treasure hunters. You remember the bad guys like that in all the pictures, right? Anyway, you wouldn't think to look at him, but he was a pretty good shot with those apples too. He caught one guy square on the jaw and knocked him right down on his backside. It was a good thing Sam Rawlings came along when he did or somebody may have gotten hurt."

"Sam Rawlings!" Frankie's eyes lit up at the name of his mentor, "Curly, you remember me telling you about Sam Rawlings. What did Tarzan do Officer Carson, when he saw Sam Rawlings?"

"Well, he takes one look at Sam and calls him '*Chief.*' '*Chief*' says Tarzan, '*Tarzan need help fighting white hunters. You go to village, bring back warriors. We fight together.*'"

"What did Sam do?"

"He thought on his feet. He tells Tarzan, *'Come with Chief back to village, together we bring back warriors. In meantime leave white hunters to get lost in jungle. Then, Tarzan and Chief and warriors come back and drive the rest away for good'.*"

"Did that work, did Tarzan fall for it?"

"I think it would've worked. Tarzan dropped his apples and had started to walk with Sam, when he saw something that stopped him in his tracks. All of this took place right in front of the town library, and Miss Postelwaite the librarian, you remember her, heard the commotion and stepped outside to see what it was all about. Tarzan took one look at her and let out one of those calls of his."

"The librarian eh?" Frankie asked "This Tarzan fellow must go for the bookish type."

"Hmm? Well no, I don't think that's it exactly, it's just that she was the first woman he happened to see. Besides, Miss Postelwaite isn't what most people think of when they hear librarian, she's really an attractive woman. She's on the tall side, slender, not exactly curvaceous, but no slouch either, and a pretty face with nice eyes. Only trouble is, her eyes and most of her face are hidden behind those imposing looking glasses she wears."

"I know what you mean," Frankie added, "Sometimes I think half the librarians in existence are really pin-up girls in disguise, and they just wear those glasses to keep the male customers at bay."

"Must be a part of their training," Phil said, "like learning the Dewey Decimal system. Upon graduation, all of the future librarians are given one of those rubber stamps with dates you can change, an ink pad, and a pair of regulation, male-proof eyeglasses."

"Sure Phil, only don't interrupt so much. And then what happened?" Asked Frankie.

"Well, let's see, where was I?"

"You left off just as your comely librarian, Miss Postelwaite popped out to see what all the ruckus was about, when this goofy guy who thought he was Tarzan caught an eye full of her."

"Yeah, that' it. Well, like I said, he see's her and let's out one of those yells like in the movies, only not nearly so well as Johnny Weissmuller does it, and calls out to her *'Jane!* "and then he pounds his fists to his chest and shouts out *"Me Tarzan, you Jane,'* and off he goes, full speed ahead, straight for Miss Postelwaite."

"What did she do?"

"Well, you can imagine her surprise. No librarian, accustomed to the quiet, ordered tranquility of her daily routine among the books and scholars likes to have her morning disrupted by a roly poly man in his underwear. She took a good look to make sure her eyes weren't playing tricks on her, screamed, and turned and ran back into the library. She hid herself in the er, powder room."

"What did Tarzan do?"

"He followed her."

"Into the powder room!"

"No, of course not. He followed her into the library, where I guess he must have thought she just vanished into thin air. Anyway, he gave up the chase and walked back outside, kind of quiet and sullen. Everyone was still in sort of a daze, so no one thought to detain him. He walked down the library steps and climbed up a big beech tree, and hid himself in the branches."

"Then what?"

"Nothing. He just sat there, hidden in the leaves. I think he was brooding."

"Brooding in a beech tree in your BVD's, and all before breakfast too. The people in your town do live." Phil said with a shake of his head.

"He wasn't actually from around here." Officer Carson reminded him, "And, you've got to remember, he was suffering from amnesia, which we later found out was from a bump on the head. Give the guy credit for that."

"Yes, well, I suppose the bump on the head counts for something." Phil acknowledged.

"So how did you finally get him down?" Frankie asked.

"By this time the Chief of Police, and most of the other guys on the force were there. Some of us tried to climb the tree, but every time somebody got close, a foot would come jabbing down out of the branches and knock him back down. We didn't want to storm the tree and take him by force, because he wasn't actually hurting anyone, and we didn't want him or anybody else to fall out of the tree and get hurt. Then someone told the Chief how the guy had reacted to Miss Postelwaite, how he had called her Jane, and so on, so the Chief came up with the idea that if this guy were to see another Jane, he would come down out of the tree after her, just like he did the first time." Officer Carson's telling of the narrative slowed at this point."

""So...?"

"So, naturally the person posing as Jane would have to be a member of the force."

"Naturally."

"So, after a careful review of all the candidates and their qualifications to pull off the ruse, the Chief selected--"

"Just a moment Officer, what kind of review of what qualifications?"

Officer Carson cleared his throat. "Well, seeing as the person being impersonated was supposed to be an attractive, young woman clad in some sort of simple, short dress made of animal skin, the Chief decided that the shape of the candidates legs were important if we were to be successful in convincing the poor fellow. So he, the Chief that is, instructed all of us, that is each of the candidates, to pull up his trousers to the knee, and after after evaluating the candidates to see who had the -er shapeliest legs, he made his choice."

"And then what happened?"

"The candidate selected was fitted up with a wig, and provided a piece of costume that served as the animal skin dress."

"Yes?"

"After donning this disguise, the candidate proceeded to some bushes, from which he had been instructed by his superior to try and lure the subject with word, and if necessary, gesture."

"Word and gesture? What kind of word and gesture?"

Officer Carson cleared his throat again and resumed in a high falsetto. *'Tarzan, oh Tarzan! Over here Tarzan, it is I, your lovely Jane. Come to me, my mate!'* "

"Oh boy, that's some juicy dialogue. Did that get him?"

"It got his attention all right. A whole bunch of leaves shook and rustled like a strong wind was blowing through them, but he didn't climb down right away."

"So it was time to throw in some gestures too?"

"Yeah, so the candidate, seeing that the subject was not stirring from his roost, and upon urging from his superior, proceeded to dangle a leg- er limb, from behind the bush and in plain view of the subject, in a provocative and inviting manner."

"And did that do the trick?" Frankie asked.

Officer Carson continued, "Yes, a loud cry, like the one previously made by the subject prior to his pursuit of Miss Postelwaite, was heard from the tree, another great rustling was observed in the branches, following which a heavy object, to wit, the subject, plummeted to earth, who, immediately after regaining his footing, proceeded with all possible haste directly for the volunteer candidate The subject was intercepted and restrained without injury or further incident, by other members of the force. In the interest of modesty, and to facilitate immediate transport, the subject was quickly clothed in the orange coveralls which he had left near the scene of the incident."

"Wow," Phil gasped, "What a tale. They should've given that policeman a special citation."

"They did." Officer Carson replied. "My Mother had it framed."

"Your, Mother? Then it was you who dressed up as Jane?" Phil asked.

"And it's you who has the most shapely legs on the force?" Frankie added.

"All right fellows, all right. Now cut it out, would you? You heard me say I would just as soon people forget all about that. Now you know why. I don't like to think of that day."

"Why not? You were the one who got him out of that tree with nobody getting hurt."

"Maybe so, but dressing up and acting like that, it just isn't dignified."

"Sorry Officer, we'll drop it. Hey Frankie, no wonder those coveralls caused such a stir. Imagine what people must have thought when they saw us."

"Yeah, no wonder is right. Hey Officer Carson, what happened to Tarzan? Did he ever find out who he really was?"

"By a strange coincidence, when they were transporting him to another facility, he fell off a railway platform and bumped his head. That bump acted like magic and he remembered everything, his name, his family, his occupation, everything. He was in women's underwear."

"That couldn't have been comfortable."

"No, I meant to say that was his line. He was a traveling salesman, and he sold women's foundation garments to stores all through the region. One day when he was about to board a train, he fell off the platform and must've bumped his head, because that was the last thing he remembered until he bumped his head falling off the platform the second time. After that, everything came back to him, clear as a bell. His name is Joe Kadokes, he's really just a quiet, retiring sort of guy from Oskaloosa Iowa, and has a wife and two kids. They were glad to get him back."

"Sounds like a happy ending." Phil observed.

"I wonder what made a quiet, retiring guy choose Tarzan?" Frankie pondered.

"The docs' had something to say about that. They figured it was his occupation that caused him to fixate on that particular character."

"How so?" Frankie asked.

"They said that repressed primal urges in the docile male often find vent in the exact counterpart of that male's personality traits when the cause of the repression in suddenly removed, either by chemical means, or a physical trauma such as a blow to the head."

"*Repressed primal urges.* Did you hear that Curly? That should be a lesson to all of us."

"Well what about this Joe Kadokes, what if he ever bumps his head again? What happens then?"

"He thought of that too. He got out of women's underwear. Now he's in bathroom fixtures."

"That sounds harmless enough." Frankie said, "What kind of repressed primal urges could a guy get from selling bathtubs and er?"

"Hopefully none of us will ever have to answer that question for real." Officer Carson replied, and both Phil and Frankie nodded their heads in assent.

"Well, thanks for telling us the whole story Officer Carson, and thanks for being patient with us while you thought we were patients."

"Sure, don't mention it."

"Phil looked back towards the house, "That Mrs. Springyton. She is quite a remarkable woman."

"None better."

"So thoughtful and kind. I have to admit I thought she was a little dizzy at first, but I don't think that's the case at all."

"I know what you mean. I thought she was a little flighty when I first met her myself; but now I think that's just her way of setting a comforting tone, you know, to help others feel at ease. Although she may act like she's up in the air some of the time, I believe Mrs. Springyton has both feet on the ground, and I mean on firm, steady rock."

"I think you're right Officer Carson, there's something solid behind that dizzy exterior."

"Solid is right, and she's got a heart of gold."

"Did you say a heart of gold?"

"What's the matter, don't you think so too?"

"Oh no, it's not that at all. I agree. It's just that when you said that, it made me think of something. Something important."

"Well, I'd better get going." Officer Carson motioned in the direction opposite the way to Phil's house. "I'm headed this way, so, see you soon, Mr. Webster, Mr. Elliot."

"Just call me Phil."

"Or Curly, that's what I call him."

"Yeah, or Curly. Just don't call me Babe."

"And you can just call me Frankie."

"Okay, Phil, Frankie, it was nice meeting you. Next time you see me if I'm off duty, you can just call me Jack. Bye for now, and Merry Christmas."

"Merry Christmas." Phil and Frankie said together.

"Come on Curly, let's get out of these orange danger signs before we cause any more confusion."

"Yeah, I suppose there's no longer any hurry on finishing the rest of that snow family. You go ahead up to the house, I'll be with you in a minute. I'm going to grab that shovel."

"After we get out of these coveralls, maybe we could take Petey for a walk."

"That's a good idea. Petey could probably stand for a walk about now." Phil reached for the snow shovel and pulled it out of the deep bank of snow. "Here's how *Paul Bunyan* would swing it up and over his shoulder--"

The quiet afternoon air was disturbed by a clanging sound, as of a large, metal object striking something hard.

"Oops, guess I was a little too close to that tree."

Frankie, who had just stepped inside, popped back out. "Hey Curly, what was that? It sounded like my old man when he used to call the dogs in by banging a soup bone on a cast iron skillet."

"It was just me, Frankie. I must have hit that tree trunk with this shovel when I swung it up onto my shoulder, you know, *Paul Bunyan* style again."

"Tree trunk nothing! Look behind you Curly."

"Why? What did I--" Laid out on the ground at Phil's feet was Mr. Gordon. "Mr. Gordon! Oh no! Frankie, come here, quick, it's Mr. Gordon."

"Well *Paul Bunyan*, you felled him with one swipe of your mighty shovel."

"Frankie, this is no laughing matter. I think I killed him! Oh, poor Mr. Gordon."

# CHAPTER EIGHT

## *Rescue dogs and cats out of the bag*

"You didn't kill him, Curly. Look, his eyelids are twitching."

Indeed, if Max Fleischer were to animate this scene, we would doubtless see Mr. Gordon with a swirl of stars circling his head, while a lump visibly sprouted to mountainous proportions from his cranium, and the sounds of bells and tweeting birds was heard. Over his eyes however, there would thankfully be no tell-tale X's, the animator's sure sign of a goner. As Frankie had said, Mr. Gordon's eyelids were indeed twitching.

""r. Gordon? Mr. Gordon! Speak to me. Are you all right?"

Mr. Gordon opened his eyes and looked at Phil and Frankie. "What hit me?"

"It was me Mr. Gordon. I'm so sorry. I did it with the shovel. Oh, it was an accident. Please, will you forgive me?"

"That's all right, Mister, Mister...?"

"My name is Phil Wellbright, and this is my friend Frankie Elliott, and the only reason we're wearing these orange coveralls is because we found them in the closet and we needed some clothes to keep us warm."

"I forgive you Mr. Wellbright. I should have known better than to approach you with that tree blocking your view. I wanted to come over here to apologize to you gentlemen."

"*You*, apologize to *us*?"

"Yes. When I saw you two earlier today, attired as you are, I assumed you were a couple of patients from our nearby rest home who had wandered away. That accounts for my unusual behavior when we met earlier. After I telephoned Morning Rise, and the people there assured me they had no patients missing, I remembered that Bill Travers, who used to live in this house, had two sets of those coveralls, and that he and his brother used to wear them when they went up north. I do hope you gentlemen will forgive me."

"That's quite all right Mr. Gordon. Anyone could make the same mistake. Officer Carson thought we were from Morning Rise, and even that kind Mrs. Springyton thought so, until you called and cleared the whole thing up. Here, let us help you."

"Thank you, I think I'll sit a moment longer. I still feel a bit dizzy."

"Sure, take your time. Would you like us to bring you anything? A glass of water maybe?"

"No, thank you. That won't be necessary. I should be fine in a moment."

"You just say the word, whenever you're ready to get up, and Frankie and I will give you a hand. Take your time though. Don't hurry on our account."

"Thank you gentlemen. Your concern is most comforting. I suppose it's a good thing I didn't bring Bessie out with me."

"Bessie? Is that Mrs. Gordon?"

"No, Bessie is a very large dog, a Great Dane in fact. I don't know how she would have responded when you accidentally hit me with that shovel, She may have taken it as a deliberate attack."

"Well, I suppose it is a good thing then. I sure would hate to have your Great Dane think I was attacking you with a snow shovel."

"Bessie isn't actually my dog. I am caring for her until I find her a new home. That's something more than just a passing an interest of of mine. I suppose you could say I sort of rescue dogs and cats who've been neglected or abused, or whose owners just can't keep them anymore, and find new homes for them."

"You do that, just on your own?"

"Yes. We all have our strengths and weaknesses you know. I find that I'm not much good with people; I am actually rather shy you see, and I'm afraid that often makes me come off as stuffy and aloof; and I am also aware that my appearance, no matter how much I try to soften it, does not exactly cause people to warm up to me."

"Oh now Mr. Gordon, I don't think so at all."

"That's very kind of you to say, Mr. Wellbright, but I am well aware of the fact that I look like what some people would call a *sourpuss*."

Blushing deeply, Frankie could only say "Can you imagine that?"

"Yes, I've recently considered growing a moustache, or even," Mr. Gordon stroked his cheeks and chin, "perhaps a full beard. I am curious for your opinion, Mr. Elliott."

"You might as well, go the full shrubbery. If you don't like it, just shave it off. In the meantime, anything's an improvement – I mean, what harm can it do?"

"Hmm, the full shrubbery? Thank you, I shall consider that. However until then, I am happy to say that dogs don't seem to mind my appearance, and thanks to them I am able to do some good in my own small way. With a face like this, it is good to be an animal lover. Oh, here comes my wife."

Frankie turned and got his first look at Mrs. Gordon.. "She must be an animal lover too."

"Frankie!"

Frankie answered aside to Phil: "Sorry, it just slipped out. The last time I saw a face like that it was looking into a crystal ball at *Dorothy* and *Toto*."

Phil answered in a hushed tone, "Quiet will you? They'll hear you."

Frankie cleared his throat and spoke again to Mr. Gordon, "What I meant was, you know, common interest between husband and wife. I can just see that you're both filled with sincere benevolence."

"Yes, I'm sure. While Mrs. Gordon does share my affection for animals, she is a nurse and spends much of her spare time giving first aid classes. When she isn't doing that, she busies herself primarily in our town's arts and literature society. You know, always finding writers and poets and artists to come and give talks at luncheons." Mrs. Gordon joined the group. "Hello dear. This is Mr. Wellbright and Mr. Elliott. Gentlemen, my wife."

"Pleased to meet you Mrs. Gordon."

Mrs. Gordon nodded to Phil and Frankie, "Merry Christmas, gentlemen. Oswald, this is no time to be playing in the snow. We have a lot to do yet, and you're not even wearing your gloves."

"I wasn't playing dear. I had an accident. If you gentlemen will give me a hand, I think I can stand up now." Phil and Frankie helped Mr. Gordon to his feet. As they brushed the snow from Mr. Gordon, Phil said to Mrs. Gordon, "I sure think it's wonderful what your husband does to help neglected dogs and cats, Mrs. Gordon. You must feel pretty good, knowing you're caring for those animals until you can find them a new home. I have a dog too, Petey is his name, and the thought of him being neglected or abused would practically break my heart. By the way, I'm you're new neighbor. I just rented this house. I'd love to have you and Mr. Gordon come over and meet Petey sometime. He's a good dog, and very friendly."

"Thank you Mr. Wellbright. We'll be glad to visit you and your dog. We must have you over for dinner one night to welcome you to the neighborhood, perhaps sometime between now and the New Year. Wellbright...Wellbright? Seems I know that name from somewhere, oh well, I'm sure it will come to me. Mr. Elliott, haven't I seen you around our town?"

"Oh sure. I'm from around here myself. Just Curly here is new to the neighborhood."

"Seems you're some kind of musician, aren't you?"

"That's right. I'm sort of in between engagements right now."

"I'm glad to hear that, it means you have plenty of free time."

"Oh, well, I'm no good at giving lectures on my art, if that's what you have in mind."

"No, that's not what I was going to suggest. I'd like you to come to one of my first aid classes. We could always use an extra dummy."

"A what?"

"I beg your pardon. It's just that our local department store usually let's us borrow any of their extra mannequins to practice wrapping bandages, but during the Christmas season they never have any to spare."

"Oh, well, sure, I'd be glad to lend a hand. Or an arm. Pick a limb, any limb."

"I was thinking about doing a lesson on treating head injuries next time. Tell me, Mr. Elliott, were you by any chance ever dropped on your head as a child?"

"On my head! All my childhood traumas occurred at the other end, if you'll pardon the expression, courtesy of my old man's leather belt."

"My mistake. I guess my crystal ball must have been a little cloudy."

"Your crystal ball!"

"That, Mr. Elliott, is my wife's sense of humor. You see, both she and I do make jokes occasionally."

"Oh, well, that's a good one on me. I feel a little embarrassed now."

Mrs. Gordon seemed not to mind any further and spoke to her husband, "We must get going, Oswald; I need your help with the tree. Did you hurt your head?"

As they started to go Phil said, "Merry Christmas, Mr. and Mrs. Gordon. Just stop in anytime. You don't need to stand on ceremony with me. Merry Christmas."

"Merry Christmas Mr. Wellbright, Mr. Elliott. Oh, and Mr. Elliott, I'm sorry about my little joke about being dropped on your head. By the way, I've heard that you really are a very capable and versatile musician. I would so love you to come to one of our luncheons and play for us. You wouldn't have to give a lecture at all."

"Thank you Mrs. Gordon. I'll take you up on that. Merry Christmas." Frankie turned to Phil as Mr. and Mrs. Gordon walked back toward their house. "You know, they really are a couple of nice people. I'm sorry I called Mr. Gordon a sourpuss earlier and made that crack about the crystal ball just now. I didn't think either one of them could hear me. Guess I was wrong. I feel like a heel."

"Why don't you go tell them you're sorry? They both apologized to you, you should do the same, if you really are sorry."

"I'll do it. Thanks Curly." He called out, "Mr. and Mrs. Gordon, would you wait for me a moment? I'll be right there." He turned back to Phil, "Hey Curly before I go, do you realize you told Mr. Gordon your real name, and Mrs. Gordon knows it too, and she's always looking for writers and artists to talk at their society luncheons? I think you just blew your own cover."

"Yeah, you're right, Frankie. I guess in my panic after knocking Mr. Gordon unconscious, I forgot I was pretending not to be me. I heard the way Mrs. Gordon said she knew my name from somewhere too. Looks like I let the cat out of the bag. I need to go tell Mrs. Springyton my real name too. I wouldn't want that nice woman to find out from someone else."

"Okay Curly. I'll catch up with you after I finish telling Mr. and Mrs. Gordon how sorry I am."

"All right. I'm going to get out of these coveralls, then take Petey for that walk."

"The coveralls! I almost forgot." Frankie called to Mr. and Mrs. Gordon again. "You go ahead, I forgot something, but I'll be right there." He watched to make sure he knew which was the Gordon's house, then walked with Phil back to his house.

# CHAPTER NINE

## *Woodpecker Serenade*

With the infamous orange coveralls tucked safely back in their closet, Frankie off to the Gordon's and Petey's walk complete, Phil took a deep breath and sat down on the living room sofa. He had intended to walk back to Mrs. Springyton's and tell her his true name and offer his apologies right away, but it had been a busy day so far, and the sofa felt soft and inviting, and all that cold, fresh air makes a person sleepy.

Phil leaned back and stretched out on the sofa. As if on cue, Petey jumped up onto Phil's chest. Phil raised a hand and rubbed Petey from the head and neck all along his spine. Up and down, up and down. Petey sighed as he enjoyed this spa treatment. A few moments later the room was still. The only sound was that of man and dog gently snoring.

Phil was roused from his slumber suddenly and forcefully by a loud rapping sound coming from the front door. He sat up, scooted Petey to the floor, then stood. "I wonder who that could be?" Phil walked to the front door, stretching sleepily, and opened it. No one was there. Phil stepped onto the porch and looked around. Not a person was in sight. He stepped back in the house and closed the door behind him. "What do you think Petey? Was I dreaming?" Petey looked up into Phil's eyes. "No, that was too loud to be a dream. It felt like the whole house was shaking. You heard it too, didn't you? Why didn't you get up to see who was there?" Phil picked up the boots he had worn earlier and walked back to the sofa. He had no sooner lowered himself to the cushion than he heard it again, that same, loud, rapping. "What the...?" He left the boots and proceeded stocking footed to the door. "All right Frankie, enough fun for one--" He opened the door "day." Frankie was not there. Again Phil stepped out onto the porch and looked around. This time a person was in sight. On the sidewalk near the front of his house, Phil recognized the girl he had met at The Glass Slipper on the previous night. She was standing still, and seemed to be looking at Phil's house.

"Hello." Phil said.

"Hello again."

Phil judged the distance between where Olivia was standing, and his front door, and compared it to the time it had taken him to answer. She couldn't have gotten that far. "Did you see anyone run away from my front door just now? I was sure I heard someone knocking."

"No, there was no one else around."

"Oh. Well, thanks Olivia. Sorry to bother you. I guess I must've gotten too much snow in my ears. I'm staring to hear things."

"I know what's making that loud pounding sound, if that's what you're wondering."

"You do? What a relief." Phil looked around again. "But where? I don't see anything."

"Step out here for a moment, and I'll show you."

Phil padded down the walk, avoiding the snowy patches and stood beside Olivia on the sidewalk. "There," she said, nodding towards the side of Phil's house. What Phil saw was a large bird, about the size of a crow, clinging to the side of the house. This bird was mostly black, but with white stripes on the neck and face, and a brilliant red crest. The bird drew it's head back and hammered at the wood siding with loud powerful blows.

"Whoa, would you look at that? That must be some kind of woodpecker, but I had no idea they got that big."

"That's a Pileated Woodpecker. It may be our largest species."

"I've never seen anything like it. No wonder I thought somebody was pounding on the door. Listen to that racket. I think I'll call him Jack, for jack-hammer."

"Actually, Jill would be a better name for that one. She's a she. I just saw Jack in the trees over there a few minutes ago."

"How can you tell the difference?"

"See the crest? The red on her crest extends about halfway down the head. On the male of the species, the red extends all the way down to the forehead, and there s also a wide, red moustache."

"No kidding? Say, you really know your birds."

"I'm not an expert, but I'll need to be. My goal in studying art is to become a wildlife illustrator."

"Sounds like you've got the right eye for it, being able to tell me so much after just one look at that bird."

"You learn what to look for after studying them for awhile. Of course, it helps to have such a large subject as the Pileated Woodpecker. And with such striking markings too."

"Yeah, she sure is a beauty." Jill took off from the house and flew to the trees near where Olivia had seen Jack. "There she goes. I guess that's just as well for the house. You said that may be the largest species of woodpecker, is there some kind of debate over which is biggest?'

"Not over which is bigger, but if the larger bird even exists any more. The Ivory Billed Woodpecker is even larger than Jill there, but they're very near extinction. Confirmed sightings of them are very rare."

"It would be hard to miss a bird like that."

"Yes. I hope to see one myself next summer. Professor Riley is organizing an expedition to Louisiana to search for them. I'm accompanying the expedition in the hope that I may be able to sketch an Ivory-Billed in it's native habitat."

"Imagine that, outfitting a whole expedition just to go and look for a bird."

"It's more that just looking for it Phil, surely you understand, especially as someone with an interest in art. If you thought there was a chance that another bird, something just as beautiful as Jack and Jill there but even bolder and bigger, really existed, and you had the opportunity to see that creature for yourself, wouldn't you want to take that chance, to prove something so beautiful hasn't vanished from the earth, and, if possible, to capture a likeness of it so other people could see it's beauty too?"

"Yes, I would Olivia. It makes a lot of sense when you put it that way."

"I'm glad you agree. That's why I'm so excited to go on this expedition with Professor and Mrs. Riley."

"I wish you success in finding that Ivory...what was it's name again?"

"The Ivory-billed Woodpecker."

"Yeah, well I hope your expedition to find one is a success, and I hope you are able to bring back some great illustrations too. If they're as magnificent as you say, I'd like to see what one looks like."

"Thanks. I didn't mean to keep you standing out here in your socks so long."

Phil looked down at his feet, "What? No wonder I was starting to get such a chill. Where were you headed, anyway?"

"I'm going to my friend Alice's house. She lives right there." Olivia nodded to the Springyton house.

"Is your friend Alice Springyton?"

"Yes, do you know her?"

"No, but I met her mother and niece earlier today. I was going over there myself to explain something to Mrs. Springyton. Do you mind if I walk with you?"

"Not at all, I'd be glad if you did."

"Great, I'll just run inside and put some boots on. Why don't you step inside for a moment? I hate to leave you waiting out here on the sidewalk."

"I'm right behind you."

They reached the front porch and Phil held the front door open. Petey was sitting just inside. "Petey, say hello, this is Miss, er, say Olivia, I'm sorry I've been so familiar, but I don't think we ever did exchange our full names."

"That's okay Phil, mine is Azure."

"Olivia Azure, that's a nice sounding name. Mine is Phil Wellbright, and this is Petey."

Olivia reached down and patted Petey on the head. "Hello there Petey, nice to meet you." Petey's tail wagged back and forth, "I already knew you are Phil Wellbright."

"You did?"

"Sure, we did a section on contemporary American artists. I recognized you from your photo in one of our text books."

"Me? In a text book?"

"It's the price of success, brother."

"Wow, well, what do you know? Wait till Mom and Dad hear about this. If you knew who I was all along, why didn't you say anything last night?"

"I figured you must have some good reason for keeping quiet about your identity, and I knew if I didn't go all starry-eyed school girl on you, I might even find out."

"You'll find out in a few minutes, as soon as I get a chance to talk to Mrs. Springyton." Phil had his boots on by now, "Let's go."

Phil and Olivia stepped outside. It was now early evening, with the sky a darkening blue, and a golden glow back lighting the trees and houses to the west. "Have you known the Springyton family long?" Phil asked as they walked.

"Pretty much my whole life. I was born here, and Alice and I have been friends as long as I can remember."

"Seems like a nice town. My friend grew up here. I met him a few years ago when he was out West. He's the main reason I chose this town to spend Christmas. If it wasn't for him, I don't know where I'd be right now. It's hard to imagine any place or any people nicer."

"Don't you have a home, or folks to go to for Christmas?"

"Oh, sure. I've got a swell home, and wonderful parents too. I really miss them right now. But this was something I had to do, something I needed to sort out before I could go on living my life again. It's got to do with why I was keeping my identify from you last night, and part of what I need to explain to explain to Mrs. Springyton. I hope I she'll understand."

"If anyone will be understanding of anything, it's Alice's mother. I'm sure she won't hold anything against you, if that's what you're worried about."

They had reached the Springyton front porch. "Thanks Olivia. I have that feeling too, that Mrs. Springyton will understand." Olivia rang the bell while Phil continued. "Even though I just met her earlier today, I can tell there is something special about her. I know this may sound silly but I could just feel it, the way she spoke, the way she was so kind to everyone, the way she listened and didn't let anything disturb her good cheer. I don't want her to be disappointed in me. Just in that short time I was in the kitchen with her, she made me feel sort of-" The front door opened. The light in the hall cast a golden glow behind the woman who had answered. It was not Mrs. Springyton, but Phil could see the resemblance of daughter to mother in her features, and more than that, he could feel it in her presence as he looked at her for the first time "-wonderful."

"Hello." Her voice as she spoke those two syllables was soft and friendly, like her mothers, but also possessed a different quality as well, one that got right in amongst Phil, and stirred him.

"Hi Alice, look what I dragged in."

Alice smiled as her eyes met Phil's. "My, Olivia, you do keep busy. Is he tame, or do we need to leave him on the front porch?"

"I don't know for sure if he's tame or not, but we better let him in anyway, he's your new next door neighbor, and he's also a great admirer of your mother's."

Alice blushed. "I'm so sorry. It's Mr. Webster, isn't it? Of course mother has told us all about you."

"Sorry Alice," Olivia said, "I kind of let you in for that. I would have warned you I was bringing a civilized guest, but I had no idea myself; Phil and I just sort of bumped into each other over a woodpecker. Even though we're a couple of old friends from last night at The Glass Slipper, I had no idea he lived next door to you until a few minutes ago."

"That's all right, Olivia. Won't you two come in?" Alice held the door. "In case you're wondering what all this is about, Mr. Webster, it's sort of a running joke with Olivia and my family that she is always bringing wild and unpredictable new friends, art students, with her to meet my family and I. Of course they are all very nice people, about the wildest thing about them is the way they come in sometimes with paint on their clothes and even their faces, so it became sort of a joke with Olivia that they weren't tame, but we don't mean any harm. I hope you understand."

"Brace yourself Alice," Olivia said, "Because this is no mere student of art. Hide the silver and warn all the old ladies, this is a genuine, graduated, accredited, exhibited and certified- for- real- in- the -flesh artist. He's even in a text book."

Alice looked at Phil. "He is?"

"He certainly is, *Contemporary American Artists, 3rd Edition* , page 192. One paragraph of text with a brief biography, a couple of samples of his work, and photo of artist, with caption. He wouldn't stop bragging about it the whole way over here."

"Welcome Mr. Webster. It's an honor to have you."

"And that's another thing Alice. His name isn't really Webster, he lied about that, the low down scheming skunk."

"It isn't?"

"No, it isn't. I suppose that's one reason why he wanted to come over and make peace with your mother, before the whole town told her how she had been deceived by this varmint."

"Well, Mother's right this way, if you'll follow me, Mr.-?"

Phil started to answer, but only air came out. He stopped, swallowed and tried again, "It's Wellbright, Miss Springyton." he gasped, "Phillip Wellbright. It's a pleasure to meet you."

"Thank you Mr. Wellbright. The pleasure is all mine, only, I'm a little confused."

"Relax Alice. I'm only having fun with Phil here. He isn't at all like that. He didn't even know he was in a textbook until I told him, and then his first response was to think how pleased his Mom and Dad would be."

"Thanks Olivia, you know, sometimes you get going a little too fast, even for me. Anyway, I'm glad for mother's sake, she would be so disappointed if all those jokes were true. Mother said you and Mr. Elliot were such nice men."

"Mr. Elliot?" Olivia asked.

"Sure," Phil answered. "Frankie Elliot is my best friend. He and I met Alice's mother earlier today."

"Your best friend, did you say? Is this Frankie Elliot from Arizona too?"

"No," Phil responded, "Frankie's from right here, same as you and Alice. I told you about him a few minutes ago, remember? Frankie Elliot is the whole reason I found out about this town."

"Come on you two," Alice smiled, "I'll take you in to mother, I think she's in the kitchen. I'm pretty sure Robert and Mr. Li are still upstairs, and Dad, Celia and Mary Elizabeth were all in the living room hanging up stockings last time I saw them."

As Alice led Phil towards the kitchen, Olivia sank into a chair. Her eyes stared ahead. Gone was the boisterous look of light-hearted joking. If Phil had been asked to turn around and paint a word portrait of the emotions on her face, he may have described what he saw as sad, or overjoyed, or angry, or afraid, or most likely, a deep, uncertain combination of all four. "Frankie!" she whispered.

# CHAPTER TEN

## *Ride of the Chihuahua*

As Alice and Phil fade into the interior of the house, and with his softly spoken name fresh upon the lips of Olivia we may pause to wonder the whereabouts of Frankie. When last seen, he was on his way to the Gordon's house to offer his apologies. This mission completed in a manner that brought smiles and satisfaction to all, Frankie, after a stop at his own home, found himself again at the front door of his friend Phil. To his knock and call, there was no reply from within except the familiar form of Petey looking out at Frankie and wagging his tail. "Hi ya Petey, what's up, Phil gone out again? Okay boy, I'll find him. I've got a surprise for you too Petey, a new pal!" Frankie seemed to be cradling something inside the front of his winter coat. He lifted a lapel, revealing a pair of shining eyes set in a tiny head that was topped by a pair of tiny ears. "Petey, meet *Regalo*. *Regalo*, say hello to Petey." It is difficult to say who spoke first, and one cannot assume, because it is widely know that dogs do not read Emily Post, so suffice it to say that sounds of recognition seemed to erupt from both dogs simultaneously. "You're excited too? That's fine. You guys will have to wait till later to meet for real, without this window in between. Come on *Regalo*, I think I know where to find Phil."

Back down the walkway, to the sidewalk and along the street they went, *Regalo* snug in his lair inside Frankie's coat, and Frankie whistling a few bars of *Jingle Bells*. Frankie paused near the snow-family he and Phil had been working on. He reached into one of his pockets and pulled out a carrot, and some small lumps of coal. These he arranged as the nose, eyes, and smile of the Papa snowman and stood back. "What do you think, *Regalo*? He looks happy to me. Maybe he knows of a swell little snow puppy like you, huh? Tomorrow maybe you and Petey and Phil and I can come out here and finish the rest of the family. We just got started on Mama there." *Regalo* reached up and licked Frankie on the chin, which as far as Frankie was concerned was about the nicest thing a little dog could say to a person. "Okay, sounds like a plan. Come on let's go, right next door there."

Frankie resumed whistling and started back on the sidewalk to the Springyton house. He had just reached their walkway when the sudden impact of a snowball exploding against his back brought him to a halt. "All right wise guy--" Frankie turned. Another ball of snow, thrown with excellent aim, knocked his cap from his head. "That's going too far! Show yourself, you coward." Frankie challenged as he leaned down to pick up his cap, and, after securing it back on his head, packing a ball of snow. "I dare you, come out where I can see you, and give you some of your own."

Frankie heard a couple of youthful sounding giggles, followed by the unmistakable taunt of "*Nya-nya*" then saw two adolescent looking forms dart out from behind some trees and run down the block. "Hold on *Regalo*, here we go!" Frankie secured the dog in his coat and took off after the marauders. He ran after them, hampered by keeping one arm secured around *Regalo*, but he was glad to see the two miscreants did not seem interested in escape so much as staying just out of reach. All the better, thought Frankie, he would teach them, just as soon as he got within range. About halfway down the block Frankie followed his quarry down a turn off between two houses. There seemed to be open ground beyond, although in the darkness now, it was impossible to tell; Frankie knew only that there were no house lights. Something about this spot seemed familiar in his memory, but no time for reminiscing now, they had paused to taunt him again, and he was almost withing range. *"Nya-nya"* they put their thumbs to their ears and waggled their mitten-ed hands at Frankie.

"Why you!   I'll show you who can throw snowballs!" Frankie sprinted ahead.  The taunters waited a moment longer until he was almost upon them, then giggled and turned.  They seemed to drop instantly out of sight.  Frankie sprinted to the spot where they had paused, and realized too late why it had seemed familiar.  The ground dropped off suddenly in a steep slope. Below him, Frankie could see figures skating on the frozen pond, and he had just a moment to hear the triumphant laughter of his adversaries as they saw their trap sprung with perfect timing. Frankie tried to stop his momentum, but no good!  He balanced, wavered, then, still clutching Regalo, fell flat on his back. "Whoa, hold on *Regalo*, here we go-o-o-o!" Away he went, sliding helplessly down the slope.  The night sky was cloudless and filled with many stars.  Frankie was moving too fast to count them, and besides, they were all more or less a blur as he zipped along. He thought the hill remarkably slippery, as if the youths had prepared it by dumping pails of water over the snow to make it extra icy. *Smart kids*, Frankie thought. *Regalo* seemed to enjoy the ride. He dug himself out of Frankie's coat, turned and faced down the hill and braced himself with his front paws. He raised his head and let out a series of joyful sounding barks and howls.

"A dog!" Frankie heard someone exclaim.

"What, where?" Said another voice.

"I see it, a tiny puppy, riding his chest"

"Ride 'em puppy!"

   Frankie whizzed on through the night, like a sleigh full of presents. Regalo, like a miniature Santa Claus seemed to be piloting him. *A nice night for it*, Frankie observed as he caught a glimpse of the moon streak by. He was grateful too that the pond was nice and smooth. The sleigh ride finally slowed and came to a halt far out on the ice.

A number of faces gathered in a circle around Frankie and peered down at him.

"Look at that, what a cute dog."

"Hey mister, we would have never thrown those snowballs if we had known you had a little puppy in your coat."

Frankie remained supine. "That's all right kids. *Regalo*'s not hurt. He isn't a puppy either, he's a full grown chihuahua."

"A chihuahua? "Someone asked. "I've never seen one of those before. Look how tiny it is. May I hold him?"

"Sure, he's real friendly." Frankie helped the speaker, a girl who looked to be about 12 or 13 years old, get a gentle hold on the dog. His chest now vacated, Frankie sat up and looked around. A group of five or so young teens, some on skates, and two, he presumed the snow-ball throwers wearing winter boots.

"What did you say his name was Mister?" The girl asked.

"His name is *Regalo*."

"Hi *Regalo*." She rubbed her nose against *Regalo*'s ears and forehead, "He's so soft." The girl kept a secure but gentle grip on *Regalo* as the other kids took turns softly stroking him.

Frankie gestured at the two girls not wearing skates. "Are you the two that got me with those snowballs?"

"Yes." The girl holding Regalo answered. "Dinah threw the first one, and I got you with the second."

"You two are pretty good shots. Next time, when I don't have this little guy in my coat, I want a chance to show you how good I am in a snowball fight."

"Okay mister, that's a deal. You can even pick someone to be on your team too, so it isn't two against one."

"All right. Dinah, and er?"

"My name's Virginia."

"All right Dinah and Virginia. My name is Frankie Elliot. We're on. And surprise attacks are okay, just like you got me tonight? Right?"

"Right Mister Elliot. Fair is fair, only we won't surprise you again unless we know for sure you don't have *Regalo* here in your coat."

"That's a deal." Frankie looked around at the skaters on the pond. At the far end was a skate shed and benches, glowing beneath strands of colored lights. "You know, I had forgotten about this place, until I fell into that trap of yours."

"Do you want to take *Regalo* skating? I'm sure he would love it. You can rent some skates right over there at *Stella's Skate Shack*."

"*Stella's Skate Shack*? I don't remember that place, is it new?"

"Sure mister, this is just her second year. Miss Stella is not so old as you are."

"Not so old? Who do I look like, Father Time?"

"No, Father time has a long, white beard."

"Hmm. Well that's a good reminder to shave every day. I wouldn't want to cause any confusion among the younger set. Anyway, I'd love to stay and skate with you, but it will have to be some other time, kids. I was just taking *Regalo* here to meet a friend of mine when you two, er interrupted me. This has been a lot of fun, but I need to get going. I'll be sure to bring *Regalo* back though, and my friend too. This is his first Christmas in the snow, I'm sure he would love to go skating."

"You mean your friend has never been ice skating before?"

"That's right, not as far as I know."

"Then Miss Stella could teach him how, she can teach him to skate fancy." Virginia motioned to one of the girls on skates, "Eleanor can show you. Go ahead Eleanor."

Eleanor skated away in a circle, picked up speed, changed to skating backwards, and did a sort of leap and flip in the air and ended up skating forwards again before coming to a halt with a flash of steel and a spray of ice, back where she started.

"Very nice Eleanor, you're a regular *Sonja Henie* out there on the ice. Your Miss Stella can teach my friend Phil to skate like that?"

"Sure. She's good."

"This should be worth the cost of the lessons, just to see Phil take a few tumbles. I think I know what I'm getting my pal for Christmas: Ice Skating lessons from Miss Stella. But now, I've got to get going."

"Okay Mister Elliot." Virginia handed *Regalo* back to Frankie. "Thanks for letting me hold *Regalo*, and thanks for being so nice about the snowball fight."

"Thanks everyone. Nice to meet you, and Merry Christmas."

"Merry Christmas Mister Elliot."

# CHAPTER ELEVEN

## *Puppy-dog eyes*

Phil followed Alice into the kitchen, where Mrs. Springyton was preparing dinner.

"Hello Mother, look who's back."

"Why, Mister Webster. I'm so glad to see you. After you left earlier, it dawned on me that a single man like yourself, just moved into a new house the night before Christmas Eve, you probably haven't any place to have a nice dinner. Won't you share our meal with us? If your friend Mr, Elliott has no plans, we would love to have him join us too."

"Thank you Mrs. Springyton. I haven't any plans for Christmas Eve, that's very kind of you. But before I put you in the spot of having to change your mind, there's something I need to tell you. It's about me, something I did."

"My goodness, this sounds serious. Did you rob a bank or something?"

"Well, no, nothing like that. But I did lie to you earlier Mrs. Springyton, and I regret doing it. I feel terrible, and I came here this evening to tell you how sorry I am."

"You needn't feel terrible Mr, Webster. After all, you're here now making a clean breast of it. What did you tell me that was so bad?"

"You just said it Mrs. Springyton, my name. My name isn't really Phil Webster."

"Oh dear, and I already decorated a cookie with your name on it. I know, there's young Phillip Flanagan down the street, he always stops by for cookies on Christmas day, I'll set that one aside for him."

"No Mrs. Springyton, that part of my name is real. My first name really is Phil."

"Oh, well here's a cookie with your name on it. You might want to save it until after dinner."

"Thank you Mrs. Springyton. It's my last name that I lied to you about. My last name isn't Webster, it's Wellbright."

"I like Webster, but Wellbright is nice too. It sounds, well, *well* and light, as in the opposite of dark. Well-bright! Very nice to meet you again Mr. Wellbright. Won't you have dinner with us?"

"This is very kind of you Mrs. Springyton. You don't know how happy I am, but, I have to say I'm kind of surprised you're taking this so lightly."

"Oh, I don't take lying lightly Mr. Wellbright. Lying is a very serious matter. Just because I'm not stomping my feet and lecturing you doesn't mean I don't take lying seriously. But you've already confessed what you did and said you were sorry for it."

"Then you're not angry with me for giving you a false name earlier?"

"Angry? No, not at all."

"Nor disappointed?"

"Good heavens no. You've come to me now, with the truth, on your own initiative.   You meant me no harm by saying your name was Phillip Webster when really it is Phillip Wellbright, did you, Mr. Wellbright?"

"Please, call me Phil."

"I will, thank you.  Did you Phil?"

"Did I what?"

"Did you mean me any harm by saying your name was Phillip Webster?"

"No, of course not."

"Did you mean anyone any harm?"

"No."

"Were you giving a false name to avoid being recognized by Officer Carson and perhaps being arrested for some previous crime you had committed?"

"No.  As far as I know I don't even have any unpaid parking tickets."

"There, you see?  You recognized that what you had done was wrong, you've admitted it to the people affected by your actions, no one was harmed, and now there is no longer any reason for you to feel bad about it."

"I haven't told Officer Carson yet.  He still thinks my name is Webster."

"Hmm. You'll just have to tell him the next time you see him. In the meantime, in case he finds out, I'll vouch for you.  Any way, what I'm trying to say is I accept your apology and I forgive you for introducing yourself under a false name."

"I really don't know what to say Mrs. Springyton. You've been so kind, and we only met just today. How can I thank you?"

"You can thank me by helping Alice and I get these things ready for dinner, and letting us hear no more about the matter."

"Well, okay Mrs. Springyton. Thank you for hearing me out."

***

From the chair in the front hall, Olivia could hear the soft murmur of voices coming from the kitchen and the living room. Soft was anything but the emotions inside of her. Frankie Elliot! Was she glad to have the chance to see him again? Angry? Frightened?

Frankie had been that quiet, sweet kid ever since she had first noticed him back in the seventh grade. She had felt an instant liking for Frankie, which had continued and grown all the way through high school until it was a full-fledged affection. To many this may seem strange because she and Frankie were not even friends. They didn't have any of the same friends either, and rarely even spoke to each other, except when circumstances dictated, such as that time Frankie helped Olivia when her inkwell spilled over and threatened to ruin her art project, and that other time when she had helped him when he got his tie caught in the pencil sharpener. As rare and fleeting as these moments were however, they made a lasting impression on a girl with an artistic temperament, and deep and steady emotions. There were also the looks Frankie had given her over the years. These may be described broadly as puppy-dog eyes, for Frankie was indeed a sad-looking youth who was possessed of large, expressive eyes. At least that's the way he looked to Olivia. Frankie's puppy-dog eyes were the saddest of all, because they were clearly not the eyes of the puppy that wins hearts, the one that gets taken home in a basket with a red ribbon around it. They were the eyes of the puppy that gets left behind, the last of the litter, wondering if he will ever find someone to call him their own. Starting sometime in tenth grade, Olivia's heart had cried out to Frankie, trying to offer him encouragement; surely he could sense the softness in her manner, the way she always lingered whenever he was around, but he had not seemed to notice, he merely went on looking and being shy and blushing every time her eyes met his.

Then at last there was that time their senior year of high school, at the spring dance, when she had seen Frankie approaching her, a strange look of courage and determination in his eyes. Could this be the moment he would ask her for a dance? Would this be where their fairy tale truly began? The next moment though, Bob Parker was standing in front of her, offering her a candied apple. Candied apples in high school! After dismissing him with a quick no thank you, and waiting impatiently for him to move aside, Olivia was sad to see that Frankie was no longer there. She could not have known the sinking feeling he had experienced as he saw Bob Parker, strong, handsome, athletic, and popular, approaching the girl of his dreams. Guys like Frankie never stood a chance compared to guys like Bob Parker. Oh well, he had made up his mind to say something to her that night, and he had screwed up enough courage to approach Olivia at last, but it was not to be. He turned away as Bob obscured Olivia from his view. He did not wish to see them dance together. Frankie went home. Music was his solace. He held his trumpet, but in the quiet evening, did not blow. The idea of being a musician in a swing band began to form in his mind. He could travel and see new places, and play for crowds of people, but never have to meet them, or to yearn for friendship from any of them. As long as he was standing behind that horn, no one would ever know how alone he felt.

The remainder of their senior year passed in something of a daze for both Frankie and Olivia, he planning his departure from the town of his youth, picking up all the last minute knowledge he could from Sam Rawlings, and even asking for the names of any bandleaders Sam might know who would be willing to take a chance on a newcomer like Frankie, and Olivia experiencing a welter of emotions. First there was the sadness at seeing Frankie, so obviously about to make a decisive move at last, frustrated in the moment of truth. Then there was annoyance at Frankie for giving up too easily. After all, a sad puppy-dog expression and retiring demeanor are all very attractive qualities to a girl of Olivia's creative and sensitive spirit, but there are times when what even the most creative and sensitive of girls wants is a man of action, and this Frankie clearly had proven not to be. Finally, though not a vain person by any means, Olivia felt her vanity offended. After all, when a young girl essentially sets herself aside all through seventh, eight, ninth, tenth, eleventh and twelfth grade, for that one young man who in her estimation has earned the honorary title of Prince Charming, bestower of puppy-dog glances, such a girl can hardly be blamed for feeling piqued when the party of the second part fails to pay her even the most basic of admiring addresses, and to add insult to injury, disappears from town suddenly after high school graduation without so much as a fond note of farewell attached to a simple bouquet of posies. Olivia bridled at the thought of Frankie's unexplained departure. Had their years of looking at each other meant nothing to him? At times, when her anger was roused, she imagined she could see through his little ruse of innocence. Those sad eyes were all part of his method, the means he used to lure unsuspecting girls such as herself into a false sense of security. True, he had never actually trifled with her, he had never kissed her, or even held her hand, but by some strange alchemy of emotion and expectation, she felt trifled with. She burned with resentment; he had merely been perfecting his tricks on her! When she felt loneliest, Olivia imagined she could just see Frankie, a wandering *Don Juan*, traveling coast to coast giving puppy-dog looks to any number of unsuspecting, eager girls; girls undeserving of his affection, but who would soak up his pretense and fall ready victim to his make-believe charm. Why? The question burned within her. Why did you ever bother with me? Why did you seem so nice? Why did you leave without ever saying a word to me? These and a host of other *why's* floated around in Olivia's mind. Some she asked with anger, some in feigned indifference, others in pleading sorrow.

Now Frankie Elliot was back in town.

The sound of someone whistling Jingle Bells roused Olivia from her reverie. Footsteps sounded on the porch. She stood up and turned to the front door. The *why's* were still whispering and whirling in her thoughts. The man outside had his head lowered, as though he were looking at something in his coat. Olivia opened the door. The face turned up. Olivia's heart bumped up against her back teeth. "Why-" she rasped.

"Olivia! Olivia Azure, is it really you?"

Olivia shook herself, took a deep breath and tried again, "Why,-er, Frankie Elliot, what a surprise to see you!"

"Not as big a surprise as it is to see you. What are you doing here? I figured you'd be celebrating Christmas with your husband and kids."

"My husband and kids?"

"Sure."

"Who told you I was married or that I had children?"

"No one, I just naturally figured that some lucky guy, I mean, that you couldn't possibly still be single."

"I'm not married Frankie."

"You're not! Gee, that's swell. I mean, I hope it's swell for you too. What a treat it is running into you like this."

"Is it? You never seemed to notice me much."

"I noticed you all right, you just never noticed me noticing."

"Show's what you know. I noticed all right."

"You did?"

"All the way through high school. You know it's not too good for a girls confidence when the boy she's sweet on doesn't even ask her for a dance."

Frankie cleared his throat. "Speaking of dances, what do you hear from Bob Parker?"

"He's doing fine. I received a letter from his wife not too long ago. They just had twins."

"Really? Bob Parker married and twins and all. I always thought that you and he were--"

"I hardly ever talked to Bob Parker. What gave you that idea?"

"Well, I saw you two together at the spring dance our senior year. I figured once he got you out on the dance floor, he would never let you get away."

"Bob Parker and I never even danced."

"You didn't?"

"No, we didn't dance. I was waiting for somebody else."

"Oh, somebody else." It took a few seconds for that to sink in. Frankie's eyes and his whole face lit up, "Olivia, could that have been me?"

"Who else did you think, silly? I was only doing my utmost best to look reassuring."

"Gosh, you mean if I hadn't been such a dope and left when I saw you and Bob talking, that I might have had the chance to dance with you? You were actually waiting to dance with me?"

"I'm still waiting Frankie."

"Olivia!"

*Regalo*, being a Chihuahua, does not require much space, and in cold winter weather, he is nowhere more content than when curled up in tight quarters with a human companion. This is most fortunate, because the next thing he new, his quarters had become even tighter, and he sensed the immediate presence of a second human companion. There were three hearts beating close together for the next few moments, two of them in utter ecstasy and one with the philosophical observation that this was as good a way to spend the evening as any other, as long as the others left a bit of space for him to breathe occasionally.

*\*\*\**

Having listened to Phil's explanation and assured him that he was forgiven, Mrs. Springyton paused for a moment and looked at the stove. "I think we can safely leave everything for a minute or two. Alice let's take Mr. Wellbright in to meet the rest of the family."

Alice and Phil followed Mrs. Springyton into the living room. "Phil, this is my husband James, our other daughter Celia Browning, and of course you've already met out granddaughter, Mary Elizabeth. Everyone, this is our new next door neighbor, Mr. Phillip Wellbright."

Mr. Springyton was helping May Elizabeth hang stockings by the chimney with care. He stood and extended a warm handshake to Phil. "Glad to know you Mr. Wellbright. Please, make yourself comfortable."

"How do you do Mr. Wellbright?" said Celia, "My husband Robert is still upstairs, he and our guest, Mr, Li, have had a long day of travel from Washington. I think they're both getting a little rest before dinner."

"I can't say that I blame them. You're husband is in the Navy I understand?"

"Yes, he is."

"Must be a wonderful surprise for you and Mary Elizabeth, to be able to have him home with you for Christmas."

"I couldn't ask for anything more, Mr. Wellbright."

Mary Elizabeth looked at Phil with her clear, seven year old eyes, "Mr. Wellbright, didn't you tell us before that your name is Mr. Webster?"

"Yes, Mary Elizabeth, that's right I did. I'm sorry because what I said earlier today was not the truth."

"Grandmother, is that the same as lying?"

"Mary Elizabeth, Mr. Wellbright has just confessed the whole thing to me in the kitchen. I am convinced that he did not mean to tell us a deliberate lie. He just believed that for some reason, he needed to keep his real name as sort of a secret, not to hurt anybody, but as more of a surprise. Do you understand the difference, Mary Elizabeth?"

"I don't know. Isn't not telling the truth the same as telling a lie?"

The adults exchanged concerned glances. Mrs. Springyton continued, "Yes dear, it is the same, in principle, but sometimes, when people don't tell the truth, you have to find out their intentions, and then decide if you trust what they've told you. I know, think of your Christmas presents. We don't tell you what you are getting before you open them, because that would ruin the surprise, yet when you ask us and we don't tell you, we aren't telling you a lie either."

"Is Mr. Wellbright a Christmas present?"

"A very poor Christmas present, I'm afraid. "Phil said, "More like a lump of coal than anything else, Mary Elizabeth."

"Nonsense Phil, now you stop that. Now, Mary Elizabeth, Mr. Wellbright is a very nice man. For his own reasons he wanted to keep his real name to himself, so he told us a pretend name earlier. Later on, he realized that what he had done was wrong, so he came here tonight and told me the whole thing, and to say how sorry he is. I trust and believe that he did not tell us a deliberate lie, and that we can trust Mr. Wellbright and welcome him into our home, and we needn't worry ourselves any more about the matter. He is not like a lump of coal or even a poor Christmas present. He is our new neighbor, and I am very glad to have him living next door to us."

"Thanks for explaining it to me Grandmother. I'm glad you say he's okay. I knew anyone who would build a whole snow-family for a girl he had never even met couldn't really be bad. He is like a Christmas present and I'm glad he's here too." Mary Elizabeth stepped forward and gave Phil a hug.

"Thank you Mary Elizabeth." Phil said. "Thank you everyone."

Mary Elizabeth looked up at Phil, "Did you know Daddy brought a man home with him all the way from China?"

Celia laughed, "That's not quite it darling. Daddy brought a man with him who is from China, but Daddy didn't go to China, the man was already here, visiting our country."

"Oh. China is all the way on the bottom of the world, did you know that, Mr. Wellbright?"

"Yes, Mary Elizabeth, that's right, it is."

"My friends and I tried to dig a hole to China this summer, but we had to stop because it was dinner time."

"You had to stop? Well, how far do you think you got?"

"I think we must have been getting close, it was a pretty deep hole. I could stand in it all the way up to here." She put a hand just below her shoulders to show the depth.

"Well, maybe get an earlier start next time, and you might make it all the way through before you have to stop for dinner."

"I don't know if I want to now that I've had a chance to think about it."

"Think about what darling?" Asked Celia.

"What will keep us from falling off the earth if we dig all the way to the bottom and come out the other side? Will you ask Mr. Li how people in China keep from falling off?"

"We don't need to ask him darling. I can tell you, although it may be difficult to understand. You see, the thing that keeps everyone from falling off the earth is gravity."

"Gravity? Do they have gravity in China?"

"Yes dear, gravity is everywhere."

Mary Elizabeth looked around the room. "Where's the gravity, Mommy. I don't see anything."

"Gravity isn't something you can see, dear. It's invisible, but it is always around us, always working. Even though we can't see it, we are being held by gravity right here."

"But why do we need gravity here?"

"Why? What do you mean?"

"Well, we don't need anything to keep us from falling off; we're right side up, on the top. It's those people on the bottom of the world that need gravity."

"Yes dear I know it seems that way, but to the people on the other side of the world, in places like China, they seem right side up, and we're the ones on the bottom."

Mary Elizabeth raised her shoulders and eyebrows and ducked her chin. Her eyes looked upward to the sky beyond the ceiling.

"Don't worry darling," her mother assured her, "We won't fall off."

***

"So, what did you do after high school, Olivia?"

"I took a business course here in town, at Mr. Julian's."

"Noah Julian? How's he doing?"

"He's fine, just as nice as ever. He helped me land my first job too, as an illustrator in the advertising department of a newspaper."

"That sounds like a great job for you. I remember how you always liked art class."

"It was exciting, but the job was away from home. I actually moved away for a couple of years. It was a good experience, and I proved to myself that I could do it, and I'm glad of that, but, I don't know, something was missing. I decided to give it all up, to quit the newspaper and come back here and take my love of art to the next level. I was accepted into the Art School at the college here. I work part time now teaching at Mr. Julian's to pay for tuition, and have moved back in with Mom and Dad for the time being."

"Sounds like you've had a pretty interesting time. I'm sure glad you decided to come back. Say, I just thought of something, were you at The Glass Slipper last night, talking with a fellow named Phil about your sketches?"

"Yes Frankie, I was."

"Well, what do you know? That's my best friend Phil Well-bright, and the whole time I was a little ways behind you wondering what a lucky guy he was to be talking with someone like you, and the whole time, it was *you*."

"It is pretty amazing. I never knew you were there, or even dreamed that I would see you again Frankie. I'm glad I came back too. That reminds me, Phil is here now, he's inside with Alice and Mrs. Springyton."

"I thought I would find Curly here. He had some explaining to do to Mrs. Springyton. Shall we go in?"

"Not yet Frankie. Let's stay out here a few minutes more. You've heard what I've been doing, now tell me about yourself."

\*\*\*

"I need to get back to the kitchen. Dinner will be ready shortly everyone. Alice, can you help me with the table? Do we have anyone else?"

Alice looked around. "Olivia is here somewhere. I thought she was right behind us."

"You know, something just dawned on me that happened a little while ago, right after you met Olivia and I at the door. Frankie was telling me about a girl he had a crush on when he was growing up here, right up until he left town, and by the strangest coincidence, this girls name was Olivia, and then back there, Olivia was asking about Frankie, and that's when we lost her, when she found out my friend Frankie's full name is Frankie Elliot."

Alice turned to Mrs. Springyton, "Mother, is it all right if I help with the table in just a moment?"

"All right dear. I'll make the food, you set the places, There is enough for everyone." Mrs. Springyton smiled and returned to the kitchen.

"Phil, do you suppose Olivia is Frankie's Olivia?"

"That's what I was just wondering. Frankie said he figured Olivia would be married to some lucky fellow by now, but wouldn't it be something if she turned out to be your friend Olivia?"

"Maybe that explains why she didn't come with us into the kitchen, after you told her Frankie's full name."

"Are you thinking what I'm thinking? That maybe Frankie is someone special to Olivia too. All this time, and he never even knew it?"

"I don't know. I've never heard her talk about any particular boy with special interest. I always thought she was either too serious or too busy to be bothered with romance."

"Or maybe she is just the strong type who pines away in silence, never letting her disappointment be known?""

"Olivia, pining? The thought never occurred to me. Oh, Phil, let's go find her. She was right there in the hall."

Phil followed Alice to the front hall. The door was there. The hall was there. The chair by the door was there. Even the mirror on the closet was there. The only thing missing was Olivia. Phil looked at Alice. Alice looked at Phil. They raised their eyebrows. In the short amount of time he had spent in the Springyton household, he had experienced many things, and found inside himself a growing awareness of the desire to experience many more, but one of the things he had not expected to experience in this home was a mystery.

Phil was aware, through exposure to motion-picture mystery films, that many, if not all, houses contained secret passages. In Phil's experience, these had always been near a fireplace or a bookshelf in some interior room. In none of these mystery thrillers had a secret passage been near the front door. Something about putting a secret entrance right next to the main entrance seemed to defeat the whole purpose. Yet there was definitely something inexplicable about a girl not being where she had been just a few minutes before. "Alice--" he began, but Alice shushed him with a forefinger to her pursed lips, while with the other hand, she pointed out the front door.

Phil followed her direction and saw what had to be either one very large person, or two persons standing close together. He nodded and backed quietly away with Alice.

"I guess that answers that." Phil said.

"Are you sure that's Frankie?"

"I'm pretty sure. I didn't exactly get a good look at his face.

I think it's Frankie, he was sure to come here looking for me sooner or later."

"Wait a minute, here they come."

The front door opened revealing Olivia and Frankie side by side.

"Well, well you two. Merry Christmas. Did you find some mistletoe hanging out on the front porch?"

Both Frankie and Olivia blushed.

"Phil, this is Olivia, the girl I was telling you about. Nobody married her after all, isn't that great?"

"Wonderful Frankie, wonderful. Congratulations to both of you. Frankie, this is Miss Alice Springyton, one of the daughters of our hostess, Miss Springyton, Frankie Elliot."

"How do you do Mr. Elliot, please, come in and meet the rest of the family."

"Hold on a minute! Frankie, there's something stirring inside of your coat. Olivia, I think he may have one of those Pileated woodpeckers hidden in there."

"What are you talking about Curly, this is no woodpecker," Frankie opened the front of his coat, "This is *Regalo*. I got him from the Gordons. Isn't he great?"

"A Chihuahua! He's adorable. Oh, Mr Elliot, bring him inside."

"What did you say his name was, Frankie."

"*Regalo.*"

"*Regalo*. Do you know that means *gift* in Spanish?"

"It does? What a perfect name for him. He is a gift, and on

Christmas Eve too."

"Come on to the kitchen, mother nearly has dinner ready, and I need to get the table set, but I want her to meet Regalo first."

They followed Alice into the kitchen. "Mother, we found Olivia, and Mr. Elliot out on the front porch, and Mr. Elliot brought a new friend with him.

"All right dear, just set another place at the table."

"It isn't that kind of friend. Here, take a look."

Mrs. Springyton turned form the oven. Alice nodded towards Regalo, who had his head sticking out from the front of Frankie's coat.

"Oh my goodness, a Chihuahua. What a cute little fellow. What is his name, Mr. Elliot?"

"His name is *Regalo*, which Phil here informs me means *gift*."

"Oh how perfectly sweet. This makes me think of Xavier Cugat and the rumba. I hope someone here can play a rumba on the piano. We could mix one or two in with the Christmas carols."

"I know a few rumbas, Mrs. Springyton. I'll be glad to mix them in."

"You do? Oh thank you Mr. Elliot. Now, Alice, you really need to get the table set. Dinner is almost ready."

"Right Mom. Olivia, do you mind introducing Frankie and Regalo to the rest of the family? I've got to get busy."

"Sure Alice, then I'll be right in to help with the table."

"We'll all help Alice." Phil said as he followed Olivia and Frankie to the living room.

# CHAPTER TWELVE

*Gold and light*

Olivia, Frankie and Phil were in the dining room helping Alice set the table when Celia poked her head in through the doorway, "Step lively, gang, here comes Robert, and our guest, Mr. Li The Springyton household is about to welcome our first visiting foreign dignitary. Let's make him feel welcome, he's a long way from home."

"Gosh, a foreign dignitary." Frankie said, "I sure hope I don't make a social gaff."

"Look who's concerned about social gaffs all of a sudden, the guy who doesn't even put the forks out in the right places."

"What's wrong with my forks?"

"You've got to pay attention to the way Alice and Olivia do it, and copy them, that's what's wrong. Let's just hope Mr. Li doesn't sit at one of the places you set."

"Yeah, but I gave all my forks and spoons an extra polish on my sleeve, I bet you didn't do that."

"Well, no, of course not, all of the silverware was perfectly clean already."

"Yes, but it's little details like the extra polish that make all the difference to these dignitaries. Don't you know the type? High-brow and stuffy. They like to be able to see their own reflection in their spoon." Frankie held up a spoon, breathed on it and rubbed it against his sleeve, then held it up in front of his face liked a mirror." You see, like that?"

"Olivia," Phil asked, "Was he like this as a kid?"

"I don't know, this is the most I've ever heard him talk. He was always the quiet one."

"Just chalk it up to repressed primal urges," Frankie said. "Come on, we better get going, we don't want to keep the ambassador waiting."

"Now he's an ambassador!" Phil shook his head and followed Alice, Olivia, and Frankie into the living room.

Although there may be some members of the diplomatic service of the many nations who are, as Frankie had indicated, highbrow and stuffy, Mr. Li, by all appearances, did not fall into this category. "My honored host and hostess," Mr. Li began once the introductions had been made, "Family and friends, I wish to express to you my deep appreciation for your hospitality in welcoming me as a guest in your home, especially at a time when you are gathered together to celebrate such a joyous holiday."

"Thank you Mr. Li for your gracious words," replied Mr. Springyton, "It is we who are honored to share our home with you, and it is our sincere wish that this house and all in it will contribute to making your stay in the United States an enjoyable one, and to the success of your mission here."

"I only hope that you don't mind my simple cooking after attending all those official functions in Washington." added Mrs. Springyton.

"My dear Madame, the aromas coming from your kitchen are a

delight to my senses; I can hardly wait to taste the fare which you have prepared. I have been looking forward to this moment for some time. "

"Have you?"

"Yes, after weeks of dining on board ships, and in fine hotels, and restaurants and as you said, official functions, at last a real home cooked meal! This will be my first since the dinner my own wife prepared the night before I sailed for America."

"Oh, Mr. Li, I just thought of something terrible I almost did."

"Please dear Madame, I hope you are not troubled on my account."

"No, not at all. It's just that, well we sometimes order take out food from the Chinese restaurant here in town on Christmas Eve, and I was unsure if I should do that again this year, or make a meal myself. I didn't know which you would prefer, what if you didn't like American cooking? I'm so glad I decided not to order take out."

Mr. Li let out a hearty laugh. "Oh, Mrs. Springyton, that is most amusing. Imagine after traveling thousands of miles from China to America, and for my first authentic meal in an American home, having take out from a Chinese restaurant!"

"Yes, I suppose it is rather amusing Mr. Li. Thank you so much for being so understanding."

"Thank you for the concern you have exhibited. Please pardon my laughter at your story. I trust however that my forward behavior has served to, *break the ice*, and we may all relax and treat each other simply as friends?"

"Mommy," Mary Elizabeth asked Celia, "May I give Mr. Li his present now?"

"Certainly darling. Mr. Li, Mary Elizabeth has something for you."

"Really? Young lady, I am honored."

"I was going to wait until tomorrow, when everyone else gets their presents, but then I thought this would be my way to treat you like a friend right away, especially since you came from the other side of the world and don't know anyone here except Daddy. Here it is." She held out a string of cranberries looped to form a long necklace.

"How beautiful." Said Mr. Li. "What a lovely present. Where did you ever come by such a treasure?"

"I made it myself. Mommy tied it to make sure it would stay."

Mr. Li took the cranberry necklace and draped it over his head and shoulders. "I shall cherish your gift as a very fond remembrance of my visit to America."

Mary Elizabeth tugged at her mothers hand, "Mommy," she said in a whisper that was audible to everyone, "Mr. Li is nice. I like him."

"Well spoken Mary Elizabeth." Said Mrs. Springyton.

Mr. Li smiled then turned and picked up a package from the floor behind him. 'Now, if you will allow me to follow the excellent example set by your granddaughter, Mr. and Mrs. Springyton, please accept this humble gift for you and your home, as a lasting token of my esteem and wishes for good fortune for you and your household." Mr. Li held the package out.

Mr and Mrs. Springyton looked at each other, then stepped forward to receive the gift. "It's rather heavy James, better set it on the table." They took the gift to a table near the sofa and placed it there.

"Go ahead Elizabeth."

Mrs. Springyton opened the package and carefully pulled out a porcelain teapot. "Mr. Li, this is lovely. James, look at how fine this is." She carefully handed the teapot to her husband and reached in to the package and pulled out a small tea cup. "Why it's a whole tea set! Mr. Li, this is so beautiful and thoughtful of you. We shall treasure this lovely set."

Mr. Li bowed slightly. "I am happy my gift pleases you."

"The craftsmanship is amazing. I don't know if I've ever seen porcelain this delicate before."

"The porcelain industry in the city of Jingdezhen has been renowned for the quality of their craft for many centuries."

"I notice the cups have no handles. That is so different than ours."

"Yes, Mrs. Springyton. Our cultures share many values, but also have many differences. The simple tea cup may perhaps serve as a small illustration of this. While I know that many Americans prefer coffee, I do know that both of our peoples enjoy tea as well, yet, as you can see, in China we serve it differently that do your people in America. Whether we drink our tea from a cup with a handle, or without, let us share and enjoy it in good fellowship with our loved ones and guests. Is this principle not the same in both of our lands?"

"It is, Mr. Li, and I am glad we share this in common, not only our people, but you and all of us. I am very happy to have you here with us for Christmas."

"Thank you, Mrs. Springyton."

"And now, I believe dinner is ready. James?"

Mr. Springyton took Mr. Li gently by the arm. "If you will come with me, the dining room is right through here."

Everyone followed Mr. Springyton and Mr. Li into the dining room and took their places at the table. Frankie could not resist a smug glance at Phil when Mr. Li complimented the way the table was set, and how beautifully the silverware shined.

Mr. Springyton waited until everyone was seated and settled, then bowed his head and said grace. His *Amen* was echoed by all present.

Phil took a deep breath. He was glad to be seated next to Alice. He didn't know if she, or anyone had planned it that way, but if felt good to be next to her. He noticed the smile and flush on Frankie's face at his place next to Olivia. Everyone seemed to fit in and to feel at home. Even Mr. Li, thousands of miles from his home and family, in a country of a strange language and strange customs, seemed to be made to be sitting there at that table on that night.

The candles in the two candlesticks in the centerpiece of the table cast a warm glow. Phil found himself attracted to their golden light. As he slowly ate his own dinner, his consciousness slipped into a state like a waking reverie. He heard other voices, even his own voice occasionally, the sound of a fork or knife on a plate, but more and more he found himself drawn into the world created by the golden glow of those flames. They were warm and pure and bright. With each breath that Phil exhaled he seemed to feel some of the cynicism and ugliness that he had felt growing inside of him fall away; and with each intake of new breath, he felt replenished with the beauty and goodness he sensed in the world of those flames of gold, a world that represented the beauty and goodness he had found in the people in the room around him.

\*\*\*

The dinner seemed to stretch on as though there were no time. Phil did not grow weary, and he had no thoughts of anything happening beyond that table. Sometimes he would feel a thrill run through his body as Alice's arm brushed against his, or, if he turned his head just the right way and caught the gold candle light reflecting in her hair.

The evening seemed to drift from one dream sequence to another, and the next thing Phil knew, he was standing beside Alice at the kitchen counter, drying the dishes as she handed them to him from the sink. Behind him, he could hear cupboards opening and closing, and the clink and clatter of plates and silverware and serving utensils as Frankie and Olivia put things away, while the quiet, sure voice of Mrs. Springyton supervised.

A few minutes later he and Alice were seated near each other in the living room. Phil heard Frankie, from the piano ask Mr. Li. "If it isn't being too inquisitive Mr. Li, can you tell us anything about your mission, or does that fall under the category of top secret?"

"I shall be delighted to inform you, Mr. Elliot. There is nothing secret about my mission, and both Lieutenant Browning and I have clearance to discuss the matter freely. As you know our country has been invaded by Japan. We have been at war for several years now, even as your own nation has attempted to avoid war. In the event that the United States does become involved in the war, my mission here is to establish ways in which our two countries may work together more effectively and with the greatest cooperation. As I said earlier, the people of our nations share many values, but also differ greatly in many respects. My mission is to make sure those differences do not hinder our ability to work together. I am also able to give your leaders information about wilderness survival in our region. Which plants, for example are edible, what kinds of snakes are venomous, and which are harmless, and many things like this."

"The Navy and Army Air Corps are especially interested in this information, as it can really improve the chances of survival for downed aviators and air crew."

"The Navy I can understand, but surely the Army Air Corps doesn't have any planes that can reach China from a land base. Wouldn't any flights have to be launched from our carriers, provided they could get close enough?"

"That is the way it looks now, but in military planning, one must allow for the unexpected. For the time being we can do little but take into account all the possibilities, and try to plan accordingly."

"Sounds like quite an enterprise, sending our fliers, Navy or Army, on missions halfway around the world."

"I've read some of the newspaper accounts of our Flying Tigers tangling with those Japanese Zeroes. Sounds like a regular hornet's nest." Frankie added.

"Mommy, what's a flying tiger?" Mary Elizabeth asked.

"That's the name of a group of American airmen who are helping the people in China."

"Oh. Mr. Li, I hope the Flying Tigers help the people you know too."

"Thank you Mary Elizabeth. They are brave men, and are doing their best."

"Robert," said Mrs. Springyton, "Didn't the Navy have something to do with those bright orange coveralls, like the ones Bill Travers had, you know, from Morning Rise?"

"Sure, those were surplus flight gear that the Navy sold off. The color was experimental, and it worked just fine here in fresh water, but something about salt water created a chemical reaction that caused the orange dye to fade quickly, so the Navy scrapped that color and sold off all the surplus material and clothing made from it."

"Well, what do you know? We found a couple pairs of those in the closet of my house next door. You wouldn't believe the confusion they caused."

"I can imagine. Although I wasn't here at the time, I heard all about the Tarzan incident."

"Mr. Li, I'm sorry, we got sidetracked into something else entirely. Please, finish telling us about your mission. You were speaking about edible plants, and venomous snakes."

"Yes, besides sharing information with your leaders about China, a part of my mission is to learn as much about your American culture as I am able. I am even attempting to learn the newest American slang terms, so that I may share this information when I return In this way, our leaders and our people may be better prepared to understand our ally, if it comes to that."

"Do you think it will come to that?" Phil asked.

Mr. Li and Lieutenant Browning exchanged glances. "Anything that I may say in answer to your question, you would have to take as my personal opinion. Do you understand that, Mr. Wellbright? Please do not take my answer as the official position of the Chinese government, or of anything I have learned from my contact with your own government."

"Sure, I understand."

"Then, I must say that I believe it to be very unlikely that the

United States will be able to remain neutral in this conflict. Europe has been at war for over a year. The Nazis and the Soviets have conquered and divided Poland. These two powerful aggressors are currently not at war with each other, but how long that will last, no one can tell. We know that the Soviets aided the Nazis in the clandestine development of weapons after the treaty of Versailles banned Germany from doing so. Will this cooperation develop into open and formal military alliance? That is another possibility, one that frankly, concerns me deeply. Russia has a history of hostility towards Japan, and that may be one factor that will help prevent such an alliance, as long as Germany and Japan have a treaty together."

"You seem almost as concerned about the Soviets and Nazis getting together as you do about Japan."

"It is my opinion that the free countries of the world will have to face each of these hostile governments eventually. I believe the chances of defeating them one at a time are much greater than if they were to join forces." There was a space of silence for several seconds. "I hope you will forgive a guest for bringing such a sombre note to your gathering. I pray that you in America do not take your peace for granted, and that if you enter the war against the aggressor nations, that your forces will be swift and victorious. I hope that your nation does not again feel the terrible cost of war." His eyes moved from Mr. and Mrs. Springyton, to Celia, to Mary Elizabeth, and to Robert, "That no mother or father, no wife, or son, or precious little daughter must suffer the loss of their father, or husband, or son. I must tell you though, that when I see the power of your nation, and the strength and courage of your people, I must hope that through these my people may be delivered from the calamity that has come upon them" Mr. Li stared ahead at the floor.

Phil looked at Frankie and said quietly, "How about a little Christmas music, Frankie?"

"Sure." His fingers moved above the keyboard. Beautiful and soft and simple, the notes of *Silent Night* filled the room.

No one spoke for several minutes after the playing stopped. Mrs. Springyton broke the silence.

"Mr. Li, we'll be leaving for Christmas Eve service at the church soon. Would you care to join us?"

"I would be honored, Mr. Springyton."

"How about you, Mr. Wellbright, Mr. Elliot? Would you care to come along?"

"Sure." Phil answered.

"I don't know." Frankie said, " I wouldn't have to pray out loud, would I?"

"You don't have to say anything if you don't want to. You can sing if you like. There will be plenty of singing; carols and hymns."

"The carols I can handle, but I'm a little out of my league with those hymns. I'd hate to sound foolish there in a church full of people."

"Just stay close to me and you won't sound foolish. Oh dear, that didn't come out right. What I meant was, just stay by me and I'll help guide you. Just follow my lead. If you need to get my attention just tug gently on my sleeve, and if I need to get your attention, I'll nudge you gently with my elbow. Besides, if you knew half the mistakes I've made, you wouldn't worry about how you are going to sound."

"All right Mrs. Springyton, I'll go, as long as you promise to look out for me."

# CHAPTER THIRTEEN

## *Childhood magic*

Mrs. Springyton observed the crowded vestibule with a smile, "It's always nice to see the new faces on Christmas Eve."

Frankie stared around, some of the faces did look new to him, and many were vaguely familiar. Frankie saw one that was much more than vaguely familiar, and lit up, "Sam! Sam Rawlings!"

Sam Rawlings patiently pressed through the crowd and joined the Springyton group, "Frankie Elliot. Home again!"

"Gosh it's good to see you Mr. Rawlings." He grasped Sam's hand and pumped it.

"I think you're old enough now to drop the Mister. Just call me Sam, Frankie."

"Okay, thanks Mister- er that is Sam. I'd like you to meet my friend Phil Wellbright."

"How do you do, Mr. Wellbright? Merry Christmas."

"Merry Christmas to you Mr. Rawlings. Please just call me Phil."

"All right Phil, and Sam to you."

"Where is Mrs. Rawlings?" Frankie asked.

"Clara's sitting down with a friend."

"Come on, I want to say hello to her too."

"We don't have time for that right now, Frankie. I need you for something else."

"Me?"

"Sure, I need you to sit in on the piano tonight. I've got to take over on the organ. Miss Smith, our regular organist, has injured her arm and won't be able to play for a while."

"How do I know what to do?"

"Just keep your eye on me Frankie. All of the music will be right in front of you. If you find yourself in a jam, improvise, and I'll lead you out of it."

"Okay Sam, anything you say."

"I can only stay and talk for a minute or two. Robert, it's good to see you could make it home for Christmas."

"Thanks Sam. I'd like you to meet Mr. Li. He has accompanied me from Washington as part of his diplomatic mission. He"ll be staying at the house with us through the New Year."

"Mr. Li, so happy to meet you. You couldn't have asked for a better host and hostess than James and Elizabeth Springyton."

"Thank you Mister Rawlings. I have already been greatly comforted by the hospitality of Mr. and Mrs. Springyton and their household."

"Sam," Robert asked, "Do you still visit the kids in the hospital on Christmas day?"

"Yes, Robert, same as always. Would you care to join me?"

"Yes, I would, but I also would like to see if you would join me."

"What do you have in mind?"

"Well, it's just that I thought it would be a good thing to visit some of the boys at the military hospital. None of them will be home for Christmas, and it's likely most of them won't have family here to visit. I thought with your talent, we sure could brighten Christmas day for some of those guys."

"Count me in Robert. How about you Frankie, you want to come along too?"

"The kids I understand, but I don't get how there can be wounded servicemen at the hospital when we're not even at war."

"Guys get hurt, even in training." Robert answered. "With the naval base at Lake Michigan in the region, our hospital always has injured sailors and navy personnel."

"Sure, I'll tag along. If it'll brighten somebody's Christmas, count me in."

"Thanks Frankie, I'm sure you and Sam will really make a big hit. Also, while this may not be strictly according to regulation, I understand we've even had some wounded men here from the American Volunteer Group. "

"The American Volunteer Group!" Phil exclaimed, "Did you hear that Frankie? The Flying Tigers!"

"Robert, I'll leave all the details to you." Sam said, "I usually plan on getting to the hospital at nine A.M. You take it from there, just let me know where you want us to meet before we head out. For now though, Frankie and I had better get going. Merry Christmas everyone. Come on Frankie, here's an outline of the service..." Sam's voice trailed off as he led Frankie away through the crowd.

Robert turned to Phil, "I hope you'll come too, Phil."

"Me? I understand how Frankie and Sam can spread Christmas cheer with their music, but what can I guy like me contribute?"

"Don't be so modest. I heard at dinner about how talented an artist you are. Do you have any of your supplies with you?"

"Sure, I brought most of my stuff along."

"Then bring it tomorrow. You can do portraits, even caricatures of the children and the wounded men. You've no idea how far something like that can go to cheer up someone who is lonely. Just to know that someone else cares and is taking the time to visit them on Christmas Day could make all the difference. "

"All right Lieutenant, you can count me in too."

***

Alice and Phil stood outside the church. The night was clear. The sky was filled with stars.

"That was lovely, Alice."

"I'm glad you liked it, Phil."

"It's a lovely night too."

"Yes, with the moonlight glistening on the snow."

"Do you suppose it was beautiful like this, that first Christmas Eve?"

Alice looked at the sky and stars. Her upturned face moved from horizon to horizon. She breathed deeply. "I think it must have been even more beautiful Phil, more beautiful than this, or anything any of us has seen, when I think of what happened that first Christmas."

Phil looked up at the stars and sky, and watched with Alice in silence.

Mr. and Mrs. Springyton, Mr. Li, Robert, Celia and Mary Elizabeth came out of the church. "Well Phil, I hope you're finding your first Christmas in you new home a good experience."

"Yes sir. Very good. Thanks to you, to all of you, and-" he motioned around with his arms "all of this."

"It's a pleasure to have you here. You've got a good guide there," Mr. Springyton nodded at his daughter. "Alice can tell you anything about this town, or our people, that you might want to know. Well, you two take your time. If we don't see you back at the house later, Merry Christmas until tomorrow."

"Thank you. Merry Christmas Mr. Springyton. Merry Christmas everyone."

Phil and Alice watched as the others started home. After a moment or two, they both turned their faces to the sky again. When Phil lowered his gaze, his eyes met those of Alice. They smiled at each other and started walking.

"This whole night has been wonderful. How about Frankie and Olivia? Isn't that something?"

"Yes. They both seem so happy. Look, I can just make them out over there, see, walking with Olivia's parents?"

"Yes, I see them. Look up ahead. See how Mary Elizabeth keeps peeking back at us. Do you want to catch up?"

"Oh, I like this pace, if you don't mind."

"No, I don't mind. I like this pace too. This is just right."

"Mary Elizabeth probably just wonders what we're talking about. I believe you made quite an impression on her with that snowman."

"Yeah, I get it, she probably wonders what we're cooking up next."

"Maybe she thinks we're planning to build a snow castle."

"A snow castle?"

"Sure, Celia and I used to build snow castles when we were kids. They were only castles in our imaginations. Really they were just as big a mound of snow as we could make, with a doorway and tunnel through the middle to the other side, and some kind of turret attached from which we could watch out for pillaging hordes of barbarians. Celia was always the queen, and I was the princess, and master of the castle archers."

"Didn't you ever have any knights in your castle?"

"Maybe once or twice, but the boys in the neighborhood usually preferred the role of barbarian hordes. Celia and I used to make whole piles of snowballs to fend them off. I got to be a pretty good shot too."

"Really, you were pretty good pitching those snowballs?"

"Sure. Let's see if I've still got it." Alice scooped up some snow and pressed it into a snowball. "See that tree? Here goes." She took aim and threw. A puff of white appeared suddenly on the dark trunk.

"Hey, nice shot, right in the middle."

"Yes, but the tree was standing still. The boys in our neighborhood never gave me that advantage. Still, I think I managed a pretty decent average. Why don't you try Phil? See if you can hit this next tree."

"Okay. I haven't thrown a baseball in a few years, but I used to be pretty good myself. Here goes – oops, wide right. Let me try again, I think my tree was moving."

"Let me help, Phil, I just figured out what you need."

"What's that?"

"Something every kid I grew up with had a least one of before they became a good shot with a snowball."

"Okay, okay, don't keep me in suspense. When do I get it?"

"All right, Phil, you asked for it" Alice quickly reached down, scooped up some snow, and plunged it into Phil's face, "Your first face-full of snow!"

"Whoa. Brrrr, that's cold!"

She stepped back at attention and assumed an official sound-ing voice, "Archer Philip Wellbright, you have now fulfilled the time honored rite of passage of getting a snow pie in the face, and are by royal proclamation of her majesty the queen Celia, whose deputy I happen to be, to take your station among the archers of the castle. Are you ready to fulfill your duty to the queen?"

"Ready, Princess. What are your orders?"

"Yon fire hydrant doth approach too near the castle. Your orders are to see that it gets no nearer. But take care, Archer Well-bright, we are down to our last snowball."

"Our last one? Yes Princess. Well, here goes....Got it!"

"See Phil, I what did I tell you? Now, are you ready for a real test?"

"What is your command, princess?"

"I see that a nasty varlet is pursuing the young maiden Mary Elizabeth. The scoundrel thinks he is invisible, but I believe your keen eye can discern him skulking just behind her."

"What, behind Mary Elizabeth?"

"Yes, I believe if you were to take careful aim and throw softly, you could dissuade the wretch and do no harm to young Mary Elizabeth. She does love a snowball fight, you know."

"A varlet you say? Invisible too. So if I just aim for her?"

"Exactly Archer Wellbright."

"And you're sure she loves a snowball fight? Okay, softly as you say. It will take some careful aim, she's right between you sister and your mother. Here goes..."

Up ahead, a puff of white appeared suddenly a few inches below the waist of Mrs. Springyton's coat. She gave a slight start and smiled at her husband. "James dear, would you take my hand please?"

"Certainly Elizabeth, are your fingers cold?"

"James, you are so sweet."

Phil quickly stuffed his hands into his coat pockets, "I don't think I had better try that again."

"No. One miss like that is enough."

"You'll make my apologies to your mother back at the house?"

"I would, but I don't think it will be necessary. Mother doesn't seem to mind. Look at the way she's resting her head on father's shoulder."

"Like they're still a couple of young sweethearts."

"That's Mom and Dad all right."

"Yeah." Phil watched for a moment, then his eyes drifted to Alice. He cleared his throat, "Can't understand how I missed. Must have had some snow in my eyes."

"So you do, from that snowball pie I gave you. Let me brush that off. There are some loose flakes of snow on your eyebrows. Look up, can you see them?"

"Sure, I see them. They kind of sparkle in the moonlight."

"They do sparkle, I'm glad you can see it. When I was a little girl, the first time I noticed snowflakes sparkle like that I wanted to get a closer look; to see what made them glisten. I put my face down close to the snow, until I could see each individual flake. I imagined each snowflake was like a tiny town or city, and in my imagination I became small enough to walk the silvery sparkling streets. It was a magical feeling, Phil. Since then that's always been part of how I think about Christmas; it's something magical, something I can recognize and describe, but that I can't fully comprehend. Did you ever get that magical feeling about something?"

"Sure, first time I remember was out watching a desert sunset, the way the shifting rays of light changed the color of the landscape. I remember thinking as a kid, '*If I could just do something like that.*' I think that's a big reason why I started to love painting so much."

"I'm glad you've felt it too."

"I always figured all kids have some kind of feeling of magic about something, don't you, Alice?"

"I think they do. I'd like to think that every child has their own special place between pure make-believe and plain reality, the way I do for gazing at snowflakes, and you do about painting."

"You still have your magic feeling?"

"Yes, I still have mine. What about you Phil?"

"I was beginning to lose mine. I was getting used to being a big success, and was letting it go to my head. I'm just glad something woke me up in time. That's how I ended up moving next door to you, and why I took on an assumed name at first, so I could leave the big success I had become behind and reconnect with that magic I felt as a kid."

"Something like that is worth fighting to hold on to. I'm glad the struggle brought you here, next door to us."

"I'm glad too. Speaking of doors, here we are already." They stopped in front of Alice's house. Phil looked at her door, and looked back at Alice. "I think I've already found some of that magic again."

"You do?"

"Yes, and I-- Say it's hard to believe I just met you today. I feel like we've known each other a long time already."

"Tired of me so soon?"

"See what I mean? That we can already joke with each other like that , like we've known each other so much longer. As for tired of you goes, definitely not. I hope Alice, that you and I, that we, that is, that we are just getting started."

Alice hesitated. She swayed a little bit on her feet.

"I just thought of something Alice, I'm sure *Petey* and *Regalo* could use a walk about now. What do you say we gather them up and take them out for a stroll?"

"That sounds like a great idea Phil. Who knows how long Frankie will be? It is such a nice night for a walk."

"Yes, it is. You know, I hardly even notice the cold." He turned to go next door to his house.

"Did you say *the cold*?"

"Yes, that's right."

"What cold?" Alice threw her arms about herself and spun in a circle. She turned her face up. Bright, sparkling snowflakes drifted from the night sky, glittering like miniature crystals. A myriad of tiny, fleeting feather touches played upon her eyelashes and cheeks.

# CHAPTER FOURTEEN

### *Merry Christmas Alice*

Christmas morning! Phil had his gear all packed and ready to go as he looked out the window and saw Lieutenant Browning, Mr. Li, and Sam Rawlings walking from the Springyton house. "Merry Christmas gentlemen." He looked behind the three and saw Frankie approaching from a different direction, "And here comes Frankie, right on time." Phil stepped outside with the others. "Have you decided to come along too, Mr. Li?"

"Yes, I am modestly competent at playing one of our traditional instruments, the Guzheng. Fortunately I was able to bring it along on my travels. I hope that I may also provide cheer to those who are injured or ill, and are separated from their loved ones."

Unseen by Phil, Alice and Olivia came out of Alice's house and walked towards them.

Phil paused to look at the incomplete snow-family. "They look kind of sad, with just Papa finished, Frankie."

"Yeah, I guess that with one thing after another, we never got around to the rest of the family. There's Mama's base, all ready to go."

"Merry Christmas!" Alice and Olivia said as they drew up alongside.

"Good morning! Merry Christmas." Phil replied, "Are you two coming along?"

"No," said Alice, with a wink at Olivia, "I promised Mary Elizabeth to take her sledding."

"Yeah, and I said I would go too." Olivia added.

"Okay, well have fun. We'll see you later, I hope." Phil said.

"Yeah, later?" Frankie addressed this question to Olivia.

"I'll be here if you will."

Alice watched until the men had climbed into the car and driven away, "Olivia, I did promise to take Mary Elizabeth sledding, but I know something she would like to do even more."

"Are you thinking what I'm thinking?"

"I am if you're thinking about building the rest of this snow-family before Phil and Frankie get back."

"Sister, that should be a breeze. Let's go."

"Here comes Mary Elizabeth now. Mary Elizabeth, guess what? How would you like to help Olivia and I build the Mama and the sister and brother snow people before we go sledding?"

"Really? That sounds like fun. I saw Virginia and Dinah building a snow fort next door, is it all right if I ask them to help too?"

"Sure honey, bring Virginia and Dinah, bring all of your friends if you want."

"Oh boy!" Mary Elizabeth turned and ran down the sidewalk calling "Virginia! Dinah! Virginia, Dinah!"

"Alice, don't you just want to do that sometimes?"

"Do what?"

"What Mary Elizabeth is doing right now. Running through the snow, happy and yelling out someone's name."

"Go ahead, I won't stop you."

Olivia pressed her lips tightly together for a moment. "I'll do it." She filled her lungs with air, then ran off in a circle through the deep snow. "Frankie!" She yelled, "Frankie, Frankie, Frankie!" She careened back to where Alice stood and crashed into the snow. "Oh. That felt so good." She lay on her back, looking up at the sky. "Do you mind if I just stay here daydreaming for a few minutes?"

"Take your time Olivia, here come our helpers."

Olivia rolled onto her side and looked at Alice. "Alice?"

"Yes?"

"What about you?"

Alice smiled at Olivia. She too filled her lungs, then glanced at Mary Elizabeth, Virginia and Dinah, who were now quite close.

"Yes, me too."

***

It was early afternoon when Phil, Frankie and the others returned from their yuletide mission. Phil and Frankie bade the others goodbye for the time, and proceeded to Phil's house. "Would you look at that?"

"What's that Curly?"

"The snow-family. While we were gone, somebody finished the

whole snow-family."

"Wow, I'll say they did. Just like you and I planned it: A Papa, a Mama, a sister and a brother. And look they even have hats and scarves and everything!"

"I think we both know who to thank for this."

"I sure hope so, 'cause I don't want to give the kind of thank you I'm thinking to anyone but one girl."

Phil cleared his throat, "Yeah, well, you and Olivia go back a long way. Some of us have only just met a certain person."

"She likes you Curly, I can tell."

"You think so, really?"

"It's as plain as the nose on that snowman's face."

Phil looked at the large carrot nose Frankie had indicated. "Really, as plain as that?"

"Plainer, if anything."

"How can you tell?"

"It's that shimmering look in her eyes, that rosy glow in her cheek. Those things are a sure giveaway."

"Maybe she is just coming down with a fever."

"Girls with a fever don't light up like a Christmas tree every time they are near a certain someone and inch closer to him. Girls with a fever droop, and want to be left alone."

"Gosh. Frankie. This is almost too good to be true."

"You and I both, brother."

"What are we going to do about it?"

"First thing is, you tell me, is this the real thing you were talking about yesterday, you know, with the spark?"

"Frankie, all I can say is, don't let me get too near any combustible materials or there's likely to be a reaction."

"Okay Curly, then I say we go fetch our pooches, take them for a walk, and get back to that house with all possible speed."

"Come on then, what are we waiting for?"

\*\*\*

As Phil and Frankie were walking back to the Springyton house, with Petey tagging with Phil and *Regalo* tucked in Frankie's coat, Frankie noticed some colorful woolen caps sticking up above the snow fort in the next yard over. He raised his voice to make sure he could be heard, "Yeah Phil, *Regalo* here sure is a great little dog. That's one thing about a Chihuahua, you can tuck him right in your coat, just like he is now."

"What gives Frankie?"

"I want to make sure those kids can hear me."

"Kids? What kids?"

"Behind the snow fort. Don't make it so obvious we see them. See their hats sticking up?"

"Yeah, I see them. What's the deal?"

"Looks like another ambush."

"Another one?"

"Yeah, they got me good yesterday, just as I was coming back to the house. We agreed to have a rematch, with sneak attacks allowed, but, here's the point, they said they wouldn't attack if they saw I had *Regalo* with me. They don't want the little guy to get hurt."

"So what's the plan?"

"Pretend like we don't see them while we walk past into the house, then, we leave the dogs, and sneak around the back way. Got it?"

"Right. Okay." Phil raised his voice, "Yeah Frankie, he sure is a cute little Chihuahua, do you mind if I peak at him again?"

"Great job Curly, we fooled 'em."

Alice answered the door and the boys stole in. "Phil, is something the matter?"

"Everything's fine, Alice. I just have to help Frankie with something. Do you mind watching after Petey and Regalo for a few minutes while we go back outside?"

"Sure. Here Frankie, I'll take *Regalo*."

"Thanks Alice. Is there a side door or something where we can leave without being seen from your other neighbor's front yard, and loop around to the back."

"Yes, go right through the kitchen."

"Thanks." The boys crept through the house and out through the kitchen door.

Alice waited by the front door. "Alice," Her mother said, "Phil and Frankie just tiptoed through the kitchen and out the side door. Have they been having more trouble about those orange coveralls?"

"No Mother. Phil only said that he had to help Frankie with something. I'm waiting here to find out."

"Oh, well, I'll wait with you. What do you suppose it could be?"

In answer to her question, two girlish screams of delight pierced the air. A couple of snowballs whizzed past the window, followed by Virginia and Dinah. They stopped behind a tree to scoop of fresh ammunition while Frankie and Phil advanced to the wall of their snow fort from the rear. "Gotcha!" called Frankie as he took aim and let loose. Dinah ducked behind the tree trunk as the snowball narrowly missed her.

"Oh yeah?" She retorted, "Take that!" She let flee her own shot and it caught Frankie squarely in the face. He fell back into the snow, sputtering. "Curly, help me pal, it's up to you."

"I'm right here Frankie." He took aim, "For Princess Alice, of the castle archers. His shot knocked off Dinah's cap as she was reaching for more snow.

Virginia had her next snowball ready, "All right mister, you asked for it."

Phil ducked the well aimed shot, and came up with a fresh snowball. Virginia was making for some bushes near the driveway. He took aim and caught her in mid stride. By now Frankie was back up and had rejoined the fray. Both girls ran off, laughing and screaming; each snowball that caught their retreating forms brought fresh peals of delight as they dodged and stumbled away.

Phil and Frankie dusted the snow from themselves as Officer Carson came along the sidewalk. "Well," he said, "Looks like it was quite a contest. Were you two the winners?"

"Although our opponent fought bravely and well" Frankie replied, "We vanquished them from the field."

"Yes, well I can imagine what they must look like." He looked up as Mrs. Springyton opened the front door. "Merry Christmas, Mrs. Springyton."

"Thank you Officer Carson. Would you like something hot to drink, or perhaps some cookies?"

"No thanks Mrs. Springyton. I've been out on the beat for a while now, and have already wished and been wished Merry Christmas many times." He clasped his hands to his abdomen, "I don't think I could hold anymore."

"Oh, very well, then could you wait there for just a moment?" She retreated into the house and returned with a large, rectangular package wrapped in colorful Christmas paper. "Merry Christmas, Officer Carson."

"What's this?"

"Just something from our family, and the Rowling's, and the Gordon's, to show how much we appreciate you."

"Gosh, Mrs. Springyton. I never expected to receive any gifts."

"Those are the best kind, don't you think? The ones you never expect?"

"Sure, I suppose so."

"Go ahead. Open it."

Officer Carson tore the paper away and held up a hard cover Webster's Dictionary. "A full-sized, hard cover, unabridged Webster's Dictionary! Would you look at that? Why this is thicker than two triple-decker sandwiches stacked together!.

Mrs Springyton, you shouldn't have."

"Of course I should have, Officer Carson. I remembered what you said yesterday, and I realized how this dictionary could help you to be an even better public servant, and to enable you to perform your duties with the utmost efficiency and to the benefit of all of us who are on your beat."

"Well, when you put it like that, I suppose I really can't refuse." He held the dictionary with one arm and flipped through the pages. "I see some notes written here."

"Yes, well, I didn't have time yesterday to get to the store before they closed to purchase a new dictionary, and I wanted to have something to give you today, so I just wrapped up our dictionary. I will buy you a new one as soon as the stores open tomorrow."

"Gosh Mrs. Springyton, this is sure swell of you. Thank you so much, thank you too Alice. Be sure to thank Mr. Springyton, and Celia and Robert for me too. I'll be sure to tell the Rawlings and the Gordons how much I appreciate this." He weighed the book in his arms, "I don't think I can really carry a book this big around while I'm on duty."

"Just leave it here then, you may stop by at any time and pick it up."

Officer Carson handed the dictionary to Mrs. Springyton. "Okay, thanks again, Mrs. Springyton." She turned and disappeared into the house. Alice remained waiting inside the front door. "What a lovely person. There's none finer than Mrs. Springyton."

"I'm beginning to think it's a family trait." Phil said.

"Hmm." Officer Carson looked at Phil, who was looking at Alice, "Oh, yes, I see what you mean. I wish you all the best with that

Phil."

"Thank you Officer Carson, and Merry Christmas."

"You know, duty or no duty, it 's Christmas Day. I'd like to hear you say Merry Christmas Jack."

"Sure," Phil and Frankie smiled, "Merry Christmas Jack."

"Merry Christmas Phil. Merry Christmas Frankie. " He turned and looked down the street. " I see Virginia and Dinah are still lurking behind those shrubs. You two must have got them plenty riled up. Now I'll have to pretend not to notice the pot shots they take at me till they work it off. Oh well, that's all right, as long as they don't knock off my cap."

"What happens if they knock off your cap?"

"Then I have to issue them a warning. A snowball on the shoulder or backside I can overlook, but knocking off the cap, it will have to be a warning. Those girls are good shots too." He shook his head, "Well Merry Christmas again guys." He started moving slowly.

As Officer Carson walked away, Frankie called out to Virginia "Hey Virginia! Can you hear me?"

"Yeah Frankie! What is it?"

"Aim low Virginia, aim low!"

"There was a brief pause then, "Okay Frankie got it, thanks! Merry Christmas!"

Officer Carson turned back with a wave and a smile at Frankie. There was a spring in his step as he resumed walking.

Frankie bounded up the front steps and in through the door. "Hi again Alice. Where's Olivia? I hope she didn't go home."

"No, she's still here. I think I just saw her going into the kitchen."

"Thanks kid," he started to go into the house as Phil walked in through the front door, "Oh Alice, don't get too near Curly, there's likely to be a reaction." He smiled and bolted off towards the kitchen.

"What was that about a reaction?" Alice asked.

"Oh, just a little joke between Frankie and I."

"Come on in. We're just in the lull between lunch and dinner. Did you have something to eat?"

"Sure, we had a nice lunch with the guys at the hospital. What a swell group. It was just like Robert said, just by showing up there and letting those guys know they weren't forgotten, seemed to brighten their days. You should have heard Mr, Li on that instrument of his. Wow, he can really make some amazing and beautiful sounds."

They reached the kitchen just as Frankie and Olivia went out towards the living room and the piano. Mary Elizabeth was telling Mr. Li about all the different kinds of Christmas cookies, and helping fill his plate, Celia was quietly watching, and Mrs. Springyton was seated, holding a pair of trousers and a needle and thread.

"How did that turn out Phil? I didn't get a chance to ask Frankie, he whisked Olivia away as soon as he breezed in."

"Technically I think we won, but I'm not too confident in our chances if those two get the jump on us next time."

"Mr. Li was telling us that you boys already had lunch, but won't you help yourself to some cookies?"

"Thank you, they do look delicious. What did you say yesterday, Mary Elizabeth, to try the swirly kind next?"

"That's right, Mr, Wellbright. I helped Mr. Li pick out one of those, and one of these star shapes, and a chocolate chip; they're still good even when they cool down."

"Sounds like an excellent selection. I'll have the same." As he put the cookies on his plate Phil noticed Mrs. Springyton sewing, "Mrs. Springyton, don't you ever stop?"

"Stop what, Phil?"

"Stop working. Look at you, busy again."

"This? This isn't work. I'm just doing some quick repairs on some of the wardrobe pieces for the show. Their next performance is tomorrow. You weren't here to see the shows earlier in the week, were you Phil? You'll have to come with us to one of the performances this week, they close on New Year's Eve. Alice, make sure Henry and Miles take these with them if they stop by. They play *Sheridan.Whiteside* and *Bert Jefferson* in the show, Phil, you'll probably get a chance to meet them later today. There, these are finished. You see Phil, not like work at all. I only do it because everyone else seems so busy and doesn't have the time."

Aside to Alice, Phil said *"Everyone else seems busy!* I'd like to see the person who is busy compared to your mother. She is a remarkable woman."

"Thanks Phil. I think she is too."

Phil studied Alice's face. She noticed and averted her eyes, "Sorry," he said, "I didn't mean to stare."

"That's all right. I didn't think you were staring, only...?"

"It's just that I was thinking ... you resemble your mother in a great many ways."

Alice lowered her eyes.

The sound of the piano drifted in to the kitchen. Mrs. Springyton stood up. "Shall we take our cookies and go into the living room? Mr. Elliot plays so beautifully."

"Come on Phil, let's go with the others."

Olivia was seated next to Frankie on the piano bench. Phil smiled; there was plenty of room on either side, but no space between them. Mr. Springyton and Robert were seated in chairs, and *Petey* and *Regalo* were curled up in front of the fire. Mary Elizabeth made a beeline for the dogs. Everyone else flowed into the room.

"James, I was just inviting Phil to come with us to see *The Man Who Came to Dinner*. What performance would you prefer?"

"Any one is fine with me Elizabeth. I'll go more than once if it comes to that."

"Sounds like you really enjoy seeing your daughters perform, Mr. Springyton?"

"Phil, I don't know if I can describe the feeling of wonder and respect I get whenever I watch my children perform. They --"

"Hey Mrs. Springyton," Frankie interrupted, "I never did get a chance to play some rumba music yesterday. Would you like to hear some now?"

"That sounds like a wonderful idea, Frankie."

Mr. Springyton resumed, "As I said, they-"

The sound of the doorbell interrupted Mr. Springyton again.

"I'll get it." Said Robert and sprang up from his chair.

Mr. Springyton shrugged and smiled at Phil. "I'll tell you about it at the theatre."

Robert opened the door, "Merry Christmas Sam, Merry Christmas Clara, come on in!"

Sam and Clara Rawlings stepped in. Sam held the door open for another visitor. Frankie leaped up from the piano bench and started for the door, "Mr and Mrs -er, I mean Sam and Clara, Merry --" he froze as the visitor for whom Sam was holding the door stepped in.

"*Carmen Carumba*!" Yipped Frankie.

"*Carmen Carumba*!" Yipped Phil.

"*Arrugh arooo*!" Yipped *Regalo*, making three yips in all.

Carmen Carumba stood in the hall and smiled. "Merry Christmas everybody."

Frankie blinked and gulped, "It really is you! What are you doing here?"

"What's the matter, you no like?"

"Oh, that's not it at all. It's just, well, what a surprise! I just figured you'd be in Hollywood, or Brazil."

She shrugged, "Hollywood is okay place to work, but I wouldn't want to play there, not all the time anyway. And Brazil, ah, my home in Brazil is lovely, but I say to myself just this once, I want to see what a real North American Christmas is like in all the snow, so then I think of my friends Sam and Clara Rawlings, living here with all this snow, and I get myself an invitation to spend Christmas here, so here I am."

"Come on in everybody." Mr. Springyton rose and greeted his guests.

As the introductions were made and the coats taken, Frankie stepped aside with Phil. "Can you believe this is happening? We might even get rumba lessons!"

"What's this," Carmen asked, "Do I hear something about the rumba?"

"Sure," Frankie replied, "I was just going to play a little rumba music as a request for Mrs. Springyton, and I thought, well wouldn't it be nice, as long as we've got the right music, if someone here who knows the dance could sort of, you know, teach some of us who don't know, to rumba."

"You want Carmen to teach you to rumba?"

"Would you?"

"Sure Frankie," she tickled him under the chin, "You no have to be so shy about it. Come on, let's go."

"Really, right now?'

"Sure, now is good a time as any. There is the piano. There is Sam. We just got to roll up the rug brother, and let Sam play for us, and we learn to rumba. What you say Sam?"

"One rumba, coming up Carmen." Sam took a seat at the piano.

Carmen led Frankie to the middle of the living room. "Okay Sam, hit it." She held up her arms and Frankie took hold of her. "Wait a minute. What's that"

"What?"

"Your hand."

"My hand? My hand is on your back."

"I know it is on my back. That is what I am talking about. What is it doing way up there?"

"Doesn't it belong there?"

"Not for the rumba. Not the way I teach it." She moved Frankie's hand from her back to the top of her hip. "There, that is more like it."

"On your hip?"

"Sure, on my hip."

Frankie gulped. "Seems kind of funny."

"What is funny about my hip?"

"Nothing, I only meant, it seems strange to have my hand right there, on your hip."

"Is not strange Frankie, is rumba. Ready? Now we move, like this."

"I only meant, well what if a guy, with his hand on a girls hip like that, gets ideas?"

"Listen Frankie, and I will tell you something. When you are on the dance floor with someone, that is not the time to get ideas."

"No?"

"No, not if you want to enjoy the dance. The girl, she have to know that she can trust the man and he will follow the rules and be what you call a gentleman, and in my country what we call a *cavalheiro*. If a boy cannot be a *cavalheiro*, he can not enjoy the dance, and neither can the girl."

"Supposing a guy is trying to be a *cavalheiro,* but with his hand on your hip like this, he just finds himself slipping."

"Okay, Frankie. I tell you what. We play a little game. Now we are dancing on the sound stage for the motion-picture, you and I, we play the boy and girl, is just acting, okay? So your boy, like you say, he is trying to be the gentleman, but he finds himself slipping. What happens, do you you think?"

"What?"

"Maybe also his hand starts slipping a little bit too, no?"

"Probably something like that."

"Sure, just like that, it's in the script and you are the actor playing this boy, so now you let your hand slip a little lower."

"My hand?"

"That's right. Is okay, don't worry, this is just a game. I won't get angry with you."

"Okay." He moved his hand an inch lower.

"Then I move it back, like that. See?"

"Yes, yes I get it."

"Then you look at my eyes, and I smile, but I also have a look that says, *that's enough brother,* and you settle down and we enjoy the rest of the dance."

"Those rules work okay for the guys who are trying to be a *cavalheiro,* but what about the other guys, the ones who don't care?"

"Now you are talking about the big, bad wolves. I show you how the girl must deal with this kind too. Now we pretend this: you are not just the nice boy who is slipping, but you are the big bad wolf kind who does not respect me when I move his hand away. So this time your hand slips even lower, only it is no slip, it is on purpose."

"Lower?"

"That's right. Go on. You are the wolf now, remember, not a *cavalheiro*."

"Like this?--Ouch!"

The *ouch* was in response to Carmen slapping Frankie's face. He raised his hand to his cheek.

"You see Frankie, now your hand is not where it should not be. That is the rule for dealing with the men who try to make like the big bad wolf." She pulled him back and resumed dancing, "Let's continue, you are catching on very quickly. Now I want to you to forget all about your hand and my hip, and look into my eyes. See, isn't that nice? I am not giving you any ideas with my eyes, am I?"

"No, your eyes don't give me any ideas, I mean, they're fine." Frankie massaged his cheek. "Those rules pack a punch."

"Why not? You have the same rules here, do you not? A woman is allowed to strike a man to protect herself and her honor. But if a man strikes a woman, he has no honor, he is considered a low-down dirty rat, and maybe even his own friends do not want anything more to do with him, until he get himself back onto the straight and narrow path again."

"I suppose you're right."

"Sure I am right, but now, enough about the wolves and the rats. Now we just enjoy. Don't' think about anything, not the next hour or the next minute, just enjoy dancing, enjoy the music, enjoy the lights. If you are dancing with someone who is beautiful to you, enjoy their beauty. Do not think about getting ideas. Do not think at all, except to appreciate dancing with someone beautiful in your arms. *Muito bom.* Very good. Should we not be able to enjoy a nice dance like this, with someone who is nice, without anyone getting any ideas? I tell you something Frankie, you are a nice-looking boy, and Carmen likes to dance with you. So is there something wrong with that? Not if we respect each other, and enjoy the moment, and not think ahead. Maybe if you and I are already familiar with each other, maybe if we are already sweethearts, then maybe we get ideas, maybe we hold each other a little more tightly, but until that happens with someone, this is the way we do it. It is not distant and cold, maybe that is why you say before it feels funny, but it is still with respect." They continued for a few more bars. "Now, I see that there is someone here with whom you are already familiar. I see the way yours eyes glance at her, and I see the way she watch us. So, you know, Carmen does not want to break up the sweethearts, here, Frankie," she released him in front of Olivia and drew her into Frankie's arms "Now you teach Olivia the rumba, same way I teach you. Come on now who is next to learn the rumba? Mr. Li?"

As Mr. Li stepped forward, Mrs. Springyton asked, "Miss Carumba, may James and I watch and learn while you dance with Mr. Li?"

"Sure, sure, everyone can learn. Celia, Robert come on; you too Alice, Phil. Come on everybody."

"Sam," Frankie called over his shoulder, "After Olivia and I get the hang of this, I'll take over on the piano so you and Clara can have a go."

"Take your time Frankie, Clara and I have danced plenty of times. You and Olivia are just getting started."

Mary Elizabeth went and sat next to Clara. She sighed as she watched the adults.

"Would you like to try, Mary Elizabeth?"

"Sure I would, as long as one of us doesn't have to slap the other."

Mrs. Rawlings laughed as she stood up and took Mary Elizabeth's hands. "No dear, we won't have to slap each other. That was just Miss Carumba having fun with Mr. Elliot."

"Gosh. Grown ups sure have the strangest ways to have fun."

Phil looked at all of the couples dancing around him, at Sam playing piano, at the tree, the fire, *Petey* and *Regalo*. His eyes came round and looked straight ahead at Alice.

She smiled at him. "So, what kind of ideas are you getting?"

"Me? Nothing. That is, nothing that deserves a slap in the face."

Alice laughed. "I'm getting an idea myself."

"You are?"

"Yes. I'm getting the idea that this is the best Christmas I've ever known."

"Yeah. It sure it something, having Carmen Carumba show up out of the blue."

"No offense to Miss Carumba, but she wasn't the main thing I had in mind."

"No?" Phil thought for a moment, then felt his cheeks grow warm as a realization struck him. "Oh. Yeah. I think I know what you mean."

"You do?"

"Yes. I kind of have the same idea myself, Alice."

Phil had never danced the rumba before. Learning felt just as simple and easy as floating on air.

He was still floating as they danced together hours later. Many visitors had come and gone. Many smiles, much laughter, old friendships renewed and new friendships made. Candles had been lit, dinner had been served and dishes washed and dried and put away. Christmas carols were sung, more logs on the fire, pies and coffee and more music until it was late evening. In the warm light, Phil could see Robert and Celia swaying to the music, and Mr. and Mrs Springyton dancing gracefully next to them. *Petey* and *Regalo* slept peacefully by the fire. Frankie was at the piano, with Olivia leaning dreamily at his side. Of Alice, Phil could see only some of her hair reflecting gold in the light of the fire and the tree. Her head was resting on his shoulder.

Everyone else had gone or retired for the night.

Frankie ended the song and took a long slow breath.

Mr. Springyton looked at his wife and smiled, "Well Mother, I say it's time we were off to bed."

"Yes. It has been such a lovely day, James. You children will be sure to turn off all the lights, and tend the fire?"

"Yes Mother, we'll take care of it." Alice answered "Good night dear, and thanks for everything."

"Come on Lieutenant," Celia said to Robert, "Time I got you some shut eye."

"Good night everyone. When she calls me Lieutenant, I know that's an order."

Phil and Alice drifted to the kitchen as the others went upstairs. Frankie played little catches of melody while Olivia remained pressed against his side.

Phil followed Alice out through the side door onto the porch. The night was still and quiet. The sky was clear. Phil looked up and all around; he could see many stars, straight above, and all the way down to the horizon. He turned to the side. Alice had her face to the sky as well. He watched her watching in the deep blue night. There was no expression for all of that, just wonder, contemplation. Phil looked up again. The stars, the sky, the deep blue foreverness. He felt Alice and he were seeing and wondering the sames things separately, together. Was it only his imagination, or were their hands touching, holding? It didn't matter.

When he turned to the side again, it was Alice who was watching him. She smiled, then her shoulders gave a shiver. He nodded, and they walked back into the house.

Phil put another log on the fire and poked it around for a moment. He fell back against the sofa cushion next to Alice.

He looked into the fire. Gold and blue, and red flickered, orange embers glowed underneath. The warmth was soothing after the night air.

Alice nestled closer to Phil. Her hair felt soft against his cheek, each strand with it's own halo from the golden light of the fire. "It's nice, like this."

"It is." Phil took a deep breath. He put one arm around Alice's shoulder, then gently lowered his head, until it rested upon hers.

"Curled up, together, in front of the fire."

"Yes, curled up, with you."

She put her hand on his chest. "Merry Christmas Phil."

His chest rose from the touch of that hand, and at the same time, he sunk deeper into the cushion.

He could feel Alice breathing next to him.

The fire in front of him blazed evenly. It looked as though it could burn for hours.

Another fire was burning. This fire had enough fuel to last a lifetime.

By this fire he would stay.

"Merry Christmas Alice."

The End